BY THE SAME AUTHOR

A
CARELESS
WIDOW

A
CARELESS
WIDOW

and Other Stories

V. S. PRITCHETT

RANDOM HOUSE
NEW YORK

The stories in this work were originally
published in the following publications:
*The Atlantic Monthly, The New Yorker,
Vanity Fair,* and *Woman's Journal.*

Library of Congress Cataloging-in-Publication Data
Pritchett, V. S. (Victor Sawdon), 1900–
A careless widow and other stories/V. S. Pritchett.
p. cm.
ISBN 0-394-57612-8
PR6031.R7C37   1989
823'.912–dc20
89-3947

Manufactured in the United States of America
24689753
First American Edition

For my wife

CONTENTS

A
CARELESS
WIDOW

After taking a two-mile walk across fields half-way up
the headland, to break himself in, as he put it, on the
first day of his holiday, Frazier got back to the hotel.
He had a bath to get the last of London off his skin, then,
avoiding the bar already crowded with golf players, he
went out on to the terrace to be alone. He had been
coming to this hotel for three or four years in the spring,
a man who liked to stay in a place full of middle-aged
people, many of them so well-known to one another
that it was simple for him to avoid them and to be alone.
Off he went to walk all day; off they went to the golf
course or to drive about in their cars. If he was slightly
known it was by his surname: 'Frazier with an "i" he
would say with a piercing pedantic stare, giving a roll to
his stone-blue eyes as he said it, like a tall schoolmaster
mocking a boy. He was, in fact, a hairdresser who came
to this lonely part of the Atlantic coast to slough off the
name of Lionel, as he was called at the rather expensive

salon de coiffure in London, where he was eagerly sought after. ('You know,' ladies said, 'how difficult it is to get an appointment with Lionel.') He was a tallish, slender man, not one of your sunken-chested barbers, gesticulating with comb and scissors as they skate about you, grown cynical with the flatteries of the trade. On the contrary, despite his doll's head of grey hair and the mesh of nervous lines on his long face, he was as still and as dispassionate as a soldier.

At this moment, on the terrace, he was examining the distant clouds over the sea half a mile below the garden; and the few villas, watching the purple, the black, the dyed pink and the golden, as they restyled themselves in one of those spectacular sunsets common on this coast. He broke off to stretch out a hand and to glance at the palm and widely stretched fingers as if looking at a mirror. And then, after the lapse into this habit of his trade, he looked at the sky again, until the sound of the door opening on to the terrace made him turn. He saw a middle-aged woman and a young man standing there. He saw her snatch the young man's arm to reprimand him in a threatening way and then push the arm away. They moved to a table at the end of the terrace. Frazier, who preferred to be alone, thought this was the moment to go back inside, but the woman looked up as he got to the door.

'Lionel!' she called. Then she rushed at him. 'What on earth are you doing here? How extraordinary to find *you* at this hotel.'

'Mrs . . .' Frazier stood still and his eyes went wide with horror. 'Mrs Morris! I don't believe it. How did *you* find it? When did you arrive?' He pulled himself together and all those fine lines on his face switched to politeness. 'What an unexpected pleasure.'

With excitement she said: 'This is my son. He's come over from Canada.'

And to her son she said: 'Tom, I wrote to you about Lionel. I've told you how he saved my life when Alec was taken ill.'

The son was a tall, bulky young man who gave Frazier the worldly look of one more bored than surprised by his mother's habit of staring at men anywhere and, the next moment, going straight up to them and saying, 'We have met before.'

'I don't believe it, Lionel,' she said. And, almost archly, 'What a thrill!'

It would have been bad enough, Lionel thought, if Mrs Morris had been one of his customers. It was worse that she was a neighbour from the flat below his own in London whom (he thought) he had at last shaken off! Staying here! A woman who talked and talked, never finished her sentences. A floundering, overflowing, helpless widow, her face so dramatic as it shot out of her thick hair that was like an old black curtain round her cheeks.

Frazier did what he could to hide the shock of seeing her. And then he was certain she knew what he felt, for the dramatic look went. She now gazed at him humbly, guiltily, as one given to excesses of gratitude and saw the talent unwanted.

'As a matter of fact,' she said proudly, 'Tom and I are not staying at the hotel. It's too expensive. We have

3

taken a flat in one of the villas down the road. We just dine here. I used to live in these parts years and years ago. When you were a boy, Tom. We have a lot of old friends here.'

And then she laughed away the shock she had seen on Lionel's face and said to her son: 'I know what Lionel is going to do! Walk and walk. I don't know how you do it, Lionel. I can't face hills anymore. Do you know, Tom, he walks across Hyde Park twice a day to work – when he's on his feet all day! I see you going out every morning from my window, Lionel.'

'Oh,' said Frazier, ashamed now, for he liked her laugh. 'I'm sure we'll meet.'

'We're just going in to dinner. Early start tomorrow,' she said to her son. 'We're driving to Land's End.'

To escape, Lionel said he was going down the road to see what the tide was doing.

'I always like to check on the tide,' he said, as he opened the door for them and then left as they went into the dining-room.

Disaster! Friends here? I doubt it. She's on the war path, her non-stop tongue chasing him! Not staying, but dining *every night*. Oh God! His walk down to the sea was ruined. Had he let the name of the hotel slip out in those chats with her in London? At the salon he often chatted in a gossipy way about trips, hotels, countries, prices, as he stood behind his customers, feeling the heat of their scalps and seeing their torpid or fretful faces in the mirror. Women came to him to be changed, to be perfected. They arrived tousled and complaining and they left transfigured, equipped for the hunt again.

They were simply top-knots to him. When they got up he was always surprised to see they had legs and arms and could walk. He sometimes, though not often, admired the opposite end of them: their shoes.

But Mrs Morris was not a customer. She was a close neighbour, a fellow leaseholder. For him she was virtually headless, a body, a part of the building and of ordinary life. He still thought of her after the death of her husband not as a person but simply as 'the couple downstairs', giving the name of Summers, who had lived for at least ten years in the flat below and who had only one head between them – her husband's, hers being disposable from a professional point of view. To Frazier her elderly husband had looked brutally placid and she as squashed as a cushion when he went up in the lift with them. What did one know about one's neighbours in a city? Nothing, until that Saturday afternoon when his doorbell rang and rang and rang and a woman was calling 'Mr Frazier. Mr Frazier.' The porter and others called him Frazer – she had at any rate had the merit, he remembered of 'giving him the "i"'. He was marinating some breast of chicken in his perfect kitchen when he heard the bell, wearing an apron of dark blue and white stripes. He dried his hands, took the apron off and went to the door. There she was, with her winter coat open and her keys jingling from her hand.

'Mr Frazier! Please can you help me. I can't get a sound out of the porter. My husband's fallen out of bed; he's on the floor. He's had a stroke or a fit – I can't get him up from the floor. I've rung the doctor. Would you *please* help me? I am sorry . . .'

Nothing cushiony about her then. She had a tearing grip as hard as a child's on his coat and her nails pinched through to his arm; her black hair, which usually swung over her cheeks, was now pushed back from a high naked forehead which startled him by revealing the curl of a white scar on it.

'Of course, Mrs Summers,' he said (she was not Mrs Morris to him then). She dragged him to the lift but he pulled her away, saying the stairs would be quicker. He skipped down fast. She followed, more slowly, because her eyesight was not as good as his, calling out, 'He's been ill for a fortnight. He's such a weight. I found him when I came back. I went out to buy some fish because of his stomach. There was nothing in the fridge.' The door of the flat was open. He went into a thick smell, partly of spice, and upholstery that seemed vegetable and hot with marriage. He saw the open door of the bedroom – what awful curtains! – and there was Mr Summers, lying on his back on the floor with half the bedclothes dragged with him, blood on the sheet, a dribble of wet in one nostril and a pale belly with white hairs curling on it, half out of his pyjamas. The face was dark violet with a green streak in it and he had a look of disdain about the mouth. Mrs Summers was on her sharp knees beside him at once, holding her husband by the feet.

'Not his ankles!' said Lionel. He was taking the man's pulse.

'Put a pillow under his head. Pull those sheets away,' he said calmly. Frazier got his hands under the man's shoulders from behind and heaved him to a near sitting position.

'Sit up, soldier,' said Lionel. 'Hup. Hup.'

The man opened his eyes feebly.

'I'll hold him here,' Lionel said. 'You get him under the knees. Now, slowly.'

They raised the body and then let it to the floor again.

Mrs Summers stooped to pull up her husband's pyjamas. 'It's the weight,' she said again.

'Change round,' said Lionel. 'We'll get him nearer the bed.'

In the end, somehow or other, they manhandled the hot body and rolled it on to the bed, Frazier falling on top of him.

'We've got him the wrong way up. Now gently, your end.'

The man was awake now and grunted 'Bloody Red Cross.' He closed his eyes and his breathing roared.

'He was in the army,' gasped Mrs Summers, apologising. 'Were you in the army?'

'Ambulance driver,' Frazier said.

She said: 'He's been climbing the wall, all these weeks. It's those pills. I found him when I got back.'

They sat, catching their breath. Frazier looked around the room. The Summerses were a heavy couple, with heavy furniture. The head of the wide bed was padded and crossed by two awful loops of pink satin. The padded part was stained by the grease marks left by two heads. Frazier had thought of her as a cushiony woman, but in the struggle, when their bodies or arms touched, he was shocked to feel the bones through the soft flesh. Those bones must be made of iron. He saw her roughly pull her hair back from her forehead, and now he knew why he had paid so little attention to her. The hair was dull black slow-growing stuff, hanging in loose ropes – perhaps she had had soft curls when she was young, but now her hair seemed to have been set in some out-of-date perm in a style she must have settled for once and for all years ago. Her strong nose stuck out boldly beyond the weak chin, as if they were staging another wilful life behind the curtain. The face reminded Lionel of an actor he used to see in his father's underground barber shop when he was a boy. The actor's eyes were large and brown and lamplike, as hers were.

'You would have done better to have put a blanket over him and to have left him on the floor,' the doctor said when he arrived, and he called an ambulance.

Down by the sea, because the heavy weeds were hanging from the rocks, scraps of this scene came to Frazier's mind as he stood for the moment watching the tide come in quietly, making a sound of sentences without words.

Poor Mr Summers had died in hospital. A crowd of friends came to console her after the funeral. She came up to thank and thank and thank him and admired his flat and the plants on the balcony. There was a look of hunger on her face as she looked back on it when she left.

Then, after a few weeks, she was at his door, asking him with apologies, to witness her signature on some document. She was wearing a red suit as bright as a geranium – an improvement. He picked up the document and saw she had signed Pamela Morris. It turned out she was two persons, indeed three, for she was open-mouthed, eager to explain. The woman he had known as Mrs Summers had divorced a man called Morris, who had once hit her over the head with a bottle. Mr Summers had been her solicitor and had rescued her. She had met him in an hotel in Vichy when she was with her father, who lived there as a tax exile. Her tale began to ramble about Europe. At every pause, her mouth remained half open to mark the change to the next chapter, going back to Mr Morris, a man often on a yacht or at a race, while she looked after baby Tom in a house near the Lizard – 'You know the Lizard?' Which race and where was not clear to Frazier – she was calling him Lionel now. The bright red suit turned out to have been given to her by one of her rich women friends. The shoes, too. There was a moment in this talk when she became almost a customer in his eyes. No grief, no reality, her life like the shuffling of cards. The enormous distinction of Mr Summers and indeed of herself was that they had seen no point in marrying.

She paused as he got her a second glass of whisky and then said, 'What a lovely piece of cut glass. You have such lovely things.' And at this she was back to that awful night when he had been so kind, kind, kind, as if all the women in her were talking in turn. She became secretive. She repeated that she had left Mr Summers for a quarter of an hour, as she had told the doctor. But now '*not* to get fish!' He had been asleep and had suddenly woken up and asked her to fetch his wallet from his jacket hanging over a chair. He had pulled out a slip of paper. It was a betting slip. He had backed the winner in the afternoon's race at Newbury: he told her, ordered her, to go down to the betting shop to collect his winnings. Pamela Morris knew nothing about horse racing. The only quarrels she and Summers had – well, not the only ones – were about his betting. She knew he had not been out of the flat for ten days, but when she reminded him of this he boiled up in a temper and started getting out of bed. She was so frightened by his illness that she lost her head. Perhaps he *had* got out, somehow. Men did get out.

'I didn't look at the slip. I put on my coat – *you* saw me in my coat when I came up to your flat? – and went to the shop and when I gave the slip in, the man pushed it back at me. It was two years old!'

There was awe in her face as she stopped for breath: it turned into a sudden laugh hissing along her delighted teeth.

'The wrong slip?' said Lionel, who was a literal rather than a laughing man, and looked at the stretched fingers of his hand. Then he understood: her laugh showed a pride in the irresistible folly of Mr Summers. Lionel saw the first tear in her great still eyes. And, even more proudly, she said, 'I didn't want to make a fool of him in front of the doctor. Alec, you know, was a solicitor.'

As he listened Lionel became even more aware that Mrs Morris was a body. His clientele were no more than heads that he gardened as he gardened the plants on his balcony.

As he listened to her Lionel became aware that their physical struggle with Summers had created an unwanted bond. Headless she might be, from his professional point of view, but she was alive because she was deep in the belief in the plural quality of the first person singular.

Since she admired his flat – and goodness knows he admired it himself, never thought of anything else once he got home in the evenings – he showed her round it. It was not a stew of upholstery, a goulash of furniture, as hers was: every object had been picked up, collected with great care, and had had to show itself worthy: and, by the way, nothing, absolutely nothing, had come out of a boutique, nothing *outré*, jokey or licentiously odd. He showed her the perfect kitchen, installed by *himself*, and every glittering utensil.

'Alec would have loved this,' she said, conveying that it terrified her. 'He always did the cooking, never let me near the stove – never cleaned it, either. If he had a fault, he had a cook's temper.'

And she went on, in her way of begging for an answer to a question: 'I suppose that was why he was so jealous of my husband and hated poor Tom? Wouldn't have the poor boy in the flat?'

That, no doubt, was the measure of her love for the man.

They went into the two other rooms, one of which he said he was going to redecorate.

'Lionel,' she said as she looked around and then went out, 'I wish you'd decorate my flat. Tell me what to do.'

(He ignored that at the time, but afterwards her words came back to him.)

He bent down and picked up a piece of cotton from the carpet in the hall and then simply gazed politely at her without replying. He was vain of living alone. He shopped, cooked, cleaned and polished. His cupboards were models of order. His glass was polished. His china gleamed. The jars and packets in his refrigerator were labelled. If anything broke or went wrong, he himself repaired it. He took her out to his balcony where his plants thrived. He showed her the glazed cabinet fixed to his wall, electrically heated, where he grew his seedlings. Redecorate? Advise? Certainly not. She was clearly incompetent. After the death of Summers the smells of saucepans burned out on the stove in her flat came up to his kitchen. Out of kindness he gave her a small plant in a pot for *her* balcony.

That was a mistake. In a couple of weeks, she came up with the dying plant. Overwatered. She sat with him for an hour. After this she started telephoning to him, about things that had gone wrong in her flat, and then, when he evaded her, she started slipping notes under his door. Once a week he did not mind seeing her, hearing about Summers's will, or her son, Tom, but twice in a week was too much. She sat on his sofa, often in that red coat and skirt which did not go at all with his room, talking away about everyday life.

'I love sitting here looking at everything,' she said, sighing naïvely. 'You are so cosy.'

'Cosy' was not a word he liked. He was a busy, practical man, not given to idle speculation.

'You ought to have been a decorator.' (Back on her theme again.)

He said as drily as possible, struck, however, by the thought, 'I suppose I am.'

He was thinking of his work at the salon.

'Of course! That is what you are!' And she laughed.

'I was never taught to do anything,' she said, but as usual the words suggested that her life was a string of accidents, for which she had been avid, and that when these were disastrous they left an aftermath of glee. The only subject which did not end in a laugh was her son, by Mr Morris. She had 'put' him firmly into a New Zealand bank and he had left that for a job in Canada. She was proud he had done that because her ex-husband, Mr Morris, had tried to stop him. Lionel said that boys change their minds and that he himself had wanted to go on the stage.

Lionel was a listener and was unprepared when this admission made her stop talking about herself.

'Why didn't you?'

'There was a boy at school called Archie. His father was a barber, like mine. He used to act in the school play. He would draw girls' heads on pictures of Vikings in the history books – the girls in the class.'

'And did he go on the stage?'

'He was older than me. Killed in the war,' said Lionel.

'Oh!' said Mrs Morris, eager to mourn. 'And is that why you became a hairdresser rather than an actor?'

Surprised by the intimacy of this Lionel said, not wishing to talk about Archie, who had come to life in his mind, 'No, nothing to do with it. I suppose I used to watch my mother doing her hair when I was a boy. Brushing it, with all those hairpins in her mouth, putting up a piece of hair on top of her head and holding it there. It used to fall down and I had to hold it for her, because it often fell down when she picked up another long piece from the other side, then she would start winding it round – it always came out all right in the end like a conjuring trick. She wouldn't let father touch it with his scissors when short hair came in. She kept hers long until she died.'

'I know,' said Mrs Morris. 'I used to see her when Alec and I moved into the flats and she was living with you.'

'That was when father died,' he said.

'You used to take her to the theatre,' said Mrs Morris fondly. 'You go to the theatre a lot, don't you?'

Lionel was alarmed when she said this. He wished he had not revealed anything about himself. The next thing, she would be getting round him to take her to a theatre. That evening she did something very tiresome as he stooped slightly to open the door to let her out of the flat.

'Poor Lionel,' she said. 'You were so good to your mother. Not every son is,' she said. And suddenly she kissed him on top of the head, rather greedily, and having ruffled his hair started to put it right.

That was too much. She was ordinary life and ordinary life always went too far. After this he made a point of putting her off when she telephoned or slipped another note under his door. He was going out, he said. Or he was washing paint, getting the spare room ready for his sister. Also, twice after Mrs Morris left, he had to get a cloth and wipe a stain of whisky from the seat of the velvet sofa she had been sitting on, and – as he said to one of his customers at the salon – he had to hunt for days all over London for something that really got stains off velvet, and in the end he had to get the sofa reupholstered. The expense! The visits stopped. If by chance he travelled up with her in the lift he felt that too much life was going up with him and – to judge by her plaintive expression – life abashed by its longing to *frequent*.

He got back to the hotel. She and her son were dining in a distant corner of the crowded room. A long time passed before he saw them leave, and they showed no sign of seeing him. He went up to his room. 'It will be intolerable. Why didn't I ask how long they were staying? I must get out.'

He lay on his bed looking at a guide for new places.

The danger on the next morning was that he might meet her near the villas on the road before they left for Land's End. Any one of them might be the one where she and her son were staying. But once he was on the beach below and had climbed to the cliff he knew he was safe for the day; and once his feet were on the close turf his mind scattered her as his restless eyes collected all the details of the long stretch of sea and the sky like another country hanging over it. No human voices, only the screams of gulls and the hum of the wind. Below him, the sea came pouring black as whales into the deep gullies between the rocks and was sucked out like suds and then hurled in again. These walks were personal victories for Lionel after the months of piddle-paddling (as he said) around all those ladies in the London salon. Occasionally he saw other men or women walking on some higher or lower ground keeping their distance as he kept his, or – if they chanced to walk close by – sticking, as he did, to passing like solitary clouds, unmarred by a muddling word. People really were like clouds in the sky, born out of the horizon, and as the hours went by they slowly joined the rising grey populations and processions that drifted away across the blue sky and the changing sunlight. Every year he felt re-born here. The sky was always young and ageless, the rocky land got older every day. Clip-clip-clipping in the salon, Lionel also aged with every day, but here, every hour made him younger as he aged.

When he got back to the hotel at the end of a day and went into the dining-room he was relieved to notice that Mrs Morris and her son were not back. What a fuss about nothing!

And so it went on – wet or fine, he was out, on top of this promontory or that, going further every day as if daring the Morrises. Four days passed. Not a sign of them. Had he been rude? What were they doing? Was she, in her slapdash way, being almost pompously discreet? He didn't want to chat, but he would have liked to tell her and her son about some of his discoveries. For example, terror. His life had been without it: hers must have had its precipitous moments, poor sentimental soul. The paths he followed from one cliff edge to the next would suddenly zigzag and turn inland and then seaward again, around appalling ravines whose black or lichened walls dropped sheer to inaccessible spits of sand below. Gulls and crows were often at their savage wars there. Sometimes there were bloody feathers torn from dead bodies on the grass. There was one particular place, close to an estuary, where the land was in a state of débâcle: huge blocks of rocks, the size of houses or fallen castles, had been torn off the cliffs and were stranded there in a chaos of spouting water. Closer to the shore here was a brutal coagulation of stranded rock which had astonished him when he saw it on his first holiday here – a year when he had had a row with one of the stylists at the salon. The rock looked like the body of a truncated man, arms chopped short, huge chest and head tipped back so that one saw only the underside of a chin – a giant in a barber's chair, tipped back and ready for a shave. He would have liked to tell Mrs Morris about rocks. She would stretch her eyes and give one of her amazed laughs, as she always did at grotesque things made half-true: that tale of her husband hitting her on the head with a bottle and leaving the scar had been told like a wonder she had had a gift for. Had *her* chin tipped back like that?

There was one more terror, for the collector of terrors, which Lionel called 'the black wall'. It was a ravine which he studied from one side and then the other. It dropped sheer to a spit of sand left by the tide where there was a narrow isolated rectangle of flat rock, like the hull of a lost ship or perhaps a table where fifty people could sit down to eat. He had often noticed that there were boulders just below the top of the wall and from below the boulders there was a thin irregular scratched line going steeply down, vanishing behind lower boulders and then beginning again. The scratch must once have been a path used by fishermen. He stepped down a yard or two, daring himself to go down then, frightened, crawled back.

'Better not,' Frazier said, looking at his hands. They were his living. He could not afford to break his fingers or his wrists on a giddy climb like that. Anyway, he had his eye on a black cloud coming dragging rain across the sea and he had no sooner turned back towards home than a squall did blow up and whipped him and soaked him before he was halfway back to the hotel six miles away. He broke his rule and went for a large whisky in the bar.

This was on the sixth evening.

'Hullo,' said Mrs Morris's son. He was sitting on a stool at the bar with a young girl wearing jeans, his hand on her knee. She was simply pretty, with her fair hair knotted up in a careless way.

'This is Sal,' said the son. 'Mr Frazier.'

'*You* live in Falmouth?' said the girl.

'Get clued up,' said the worldly young man. 'Mr Frazier is a friend of Ma's in London. That's someone else. I told you!'

'Sorry,' said the girl. 'Oh, I know! We *saw* you this afternoon, out on the cliff.'

'Coming up from the Coffin,' the young man said. 'How far did you get? Ma dropped us on the road and we came across the fields; it's only a mile. She'd gone to have her hair done and we had to bloody walk back. We got soaked. Did you? Did you get to the bottom?

It's called the Coffin,' the boy said. 'I took Sal to look at it.'

'I didn't see you,' said Lionel. Watched!

'Ma used to take us on picnics down the path there when I was a kid, very sheltered down there. We used to have a house back on the road.' (Owning the place!) And to the girl he said: 'In Dad's time. I told you. Before they split up.' A young know-all, thought Lionel.

'Your mother took you down that wall!' said Lionel. 'It's impossible.'

'A bit dizzy, but it used to be all right. I know what you mean – you can't get down now, the rock's fallen,' the boy said.

'Will you have a drink?' Lionel said.

'I think I'd better not. Sal's soaked through and I've got to drop her. Ma will be back. But thanks.'

Lionel watched them go.

'London friend?' 'Someone else'? What did the knowing boy mean? And where on earth could she get her hair done in this part of the world, not that that would bother her!

'Well,' thought Lionel, 'that let's me off the hook. I suppose I've been rather rude to the old bird.'

He found himself wishing to see the fat woman who had got down the 'black wall' when she was young.

He went into dinner. There were two or three large laughing parties of old friends in the middle of the crowded dining-room, and murmuring grey-haired couples at other tables. Corks popped. Between courses – slow in being served because he was alone – Lionel tried to see if she and her son and the girl had slipped in and were at the table at the other end of the room. They were not. The sun had long ago gone down, and that night the fine weather broke. When he got to his room he saw his windows were drenched, and water was gushing out of the gutters above his balcony.

In the morning, the wind was steadier, the rain quieter, but the sky was dirty and the sea looked like unwashed linen. The seagulls perched on aerials and chimneys, their indignant heads turned into the wind.

That was the trouble on this coast: fogs or rain would set in for days. The guests in the hotel turned their backs to the windows and sat hiding themselves behind newspapers: the heartier ones went boisterously out to their cars. One or two little groups sat around talking about their relations in the towns they came from, in the tones of people sitting after a funeral. Every now and then a golfer would come back from the main door dispirited. Lionel sat in the coffee room, which was usually empty in the morning. An expert in choosing chairs, he had marked one down on his first day. It was now unoccupied. He kept an eye on the puddles on the terrace and saw at last that the rain was stopping.

Then he heard a voice saying to one of the waiters: 'I wonder if I could have some coffee?'

Mrs Morris was standing there carrying a raincoat and wearing a white scarf round her head. She came at once to sit with him. She had come up, she said, because something had gone wrong with the electric power at her flat.

'Would you like me to come down and look at it?' he said at once – to make amends. He had once or twice put something right in the stove she maltreated at her London flat.

'No, it's the landlord's job to see to it,' she said. And then: 'No walking today?' – flirtatiously wagging a finger at him.

She did not take her scarf off, and although her face looked bare, it looked shapely with thoughts of her own.

'We went to Falmouth yesterday,' she said. 'The trees in the harbour are much better there than here. Taller, more sheltered.'

Then, relaxing: 'Tom said he saw you yesterday at the Coffin. Mr Morris, my husband, had a house a couple of miles away once,' she said.

She laughed. 'He wanted to show his girl the place where he was brought up. Especially,' she said, 'the Coffin.'

That word excited her and then she said: 'I dropped them there. It's a mistake to go back to the past. I mean at my age. Our age,' she said. 'Don't you think?' Yet she said this with the pride of one who had always chosen the mistake when she was young, and even now she had the warm wide open eyes of a woman hoping for another.

'Tom has got a very pretty girl,' Lionel said.

'Oh, I'm so relieved he's got a girl at last – I can't tell you! I'd begun to think . . .' she stopped. 'He just wasn't interested. I mean he's twenty-nine. Not afraid of them, always about with them, but – indifferent. I was afraid it was my fault.'

'They seemed full of themselves,' Lionel said.

'He's very good at his job,' she said.

'I was afraid,' she said, 'that the divorce had upset him. Alec hated him, I told you. It was so difficult. The funny thing is' – and it was clear she thought that this, being funny, was a revelation – 'Tom liked Alec! Liked him better than his own father. Tom was really sad when Alec died.'

'He was sad for you,' Lionel said, who suddenly remembered he himself had disliked Mr Summers. The man had looked so much like the soap-white bust of someone who had never existed. Perhaps there was something sexy in the blind, bland conceit of busts?

Lionel waited. She would break off sentences as if beguiling herself with the dramas hidden beyond in the open-ended.

'You see, Lionel,' she suddenly said, 'my mother died when I was a girl, a child. Not died exactly, but "put away". I mean, I didn't know her. I'll never forget what you told me about your own mother, doing her hair. When I grew up my father used to take me abroad with him on business. Norway, Sweden, France. He had a lot of business friends. He was in timber.'

'Lonely for a girl,' he said.

'Most people thought I was having a wonderful time, but you are right, Lionel. I *was* alone half the time, sitting in hotel rooms, reading novels. The novels I read! Eating. Talking to waiters. I used to think of my mother. Mr Morris was much older than me, in timber too, a friend of father's. After him, I mean after the divorce, I was afraid of Tom's *feeling* for me.'

She looked at him greedily, intently. Lionel saw she

was working up to asking him why *he* hadn't married.

'Do you think a mother can be too frank?' she said.

Lionel was lost. He wondered if she could mean she had been chased all round Europe by her father's friends. He could see that she might have been a pretty girl, dangerous in her naïvety, either piling up day-dreams or perhaps not innocent at all.

'Was it really because of your mother you took up doing women's hair?' she said, leaning forward, avid for a secret.

'No,' he said. 'Men's hairdressing was going downhill. More money in the women's trade.'

He was about to tell her about the rock that looked like a man tipped back waiting for a shave. Her habit of rambling from the point was infectious. But she was too quick.

'Ah,' she said, with all her breath. 'Money! That's it, isn't it? You had to look after your mother. I mean you had her to live with you. I remember when Alec and I moved into the flats. We used to see you both going out together.' Then, looking around the room to see if anyone had come in and could hear, she said in a low voice: 'Alec *did* something in the law, I never understood it – one of those things solicitors are sup-posed not to do. Horses – I don't know. I mean, when he died, he hardly left me anything. Well, thank good-ness, the flat belongs to me until the lease runs out. I'm so grateful to Tom. He came over to sort things out. He thinks I should sell the lease. What d'you think, Lionel?'

What an extraordinary thing – Mrs Morris no longer

there! New people. Builders, painters, hammering. How awful.

She glowed at the surprise she had given him.

'How much of your lease have you got left?' he said.

'I must ask Tom,' she said.

'I wouldn't do it if I were you, unless you know you've got a place to go to. Prices are still going up,' he warned her. In fact, not liking change himself, he wanted to stop her.

'I don't want to be a burden on Tom. He wants me to go to Canada with him. I suppose I could, but he's very serious about this girl,' she said. 'He's fallen flat for her these last weeks. Down here! He met her with an old friend of ours. I wish I had talked to you about this before, Lionel. I'm afraid I've been very stand-offish. You must have thought I was avoiding you, but it wasn't that. We were out all the time. I've known this friend most of my life, when his wife was alive. I told him about you and Alec. But I don't know whether I'd like to go back and live in the country again. Plants die when they see me!' Her eyes were brilliant when she laughed now.

'He'd miss his garden in London,' she added, looking around the room again. 'It's stuffy in here, isn't it?' And she began fidgeting with the knot on her scarf.

'He wants to marry me, but I don't know,' she said, whether offended with her scarf or the man, Lionel could not tell. 'He's coming over to dinner tomorrow night. I would love you to meet. You always know *what to do*!'

And then she tugged off her scarf. He had been

24

looking only at a face: but now, as she shook back her hair he saw that half of what he had called the old rope had gone and that threatening parting with it. Her hair had been chopped into short curl-like lengths, her forehead was clear, her eyebrows had come to life.

'You've changed your hair,' he said. He nearly said 'You have come out into the open.' But the stylist added: 'But it's marvellous, so young.' Immediately he stopped saying 'I' and used the professional 'one'.

'One can see the ears and the neck, the forehead is rounded,' he said, and moved both his hands as if modelling the roundness himself.

'Not severe?' she said. 'Or gollywoggy? As though I'd fallen through a hedge?'

'It brings out the eyes,' he said. 'It's perfect. Slimming too.'

'You are a darling,' she said. 'I am so frightened. It shows the grey.'

It was perhaps a touch 'gollywoggy': he was silent about that. But he said a slight salting of grey gave dignity to the head.

'Now you have a head!' he said. 'I am jealous.'

'Ah?' she said curiously.

'I'm jealous of the man who did it. Where did you get it done?' he asked.

'Tom's girl friend found him for me,' she said, disappointed. 'Do you really think the forehead's all right?'

He knew she was thinking of the scar.

'Perfect,' he said. And in fact the scar did not show.

'It was rather an awful place really,' she said. 'Do you know a dog got in from the street and started eating the hair that had fallen on the floor? The poor thing might have choked to death.' She gazed. An omen? she seemed to ask.

'The time!' she said, getting up. 'I must get back. Look out of the window – there's a pair of wagtails jumping at the flies. They never fly straight. Thank you, thank you, Lionel. Between ourselves?' she said with a prudish glance. 'Don't say anything, will you?'

He walked through the foyer of the hotel to the door, where she refused to put her scarf on.

'I miss you,' she said and after a step or two she looked back at him with a pout of mock despair that seemed to implicate him in her continuing fate.

Another garrulous fragment of ordinary life was leaving him, going about its business. He was afloat in space, and below him he began to feel the cold air of an empty flat. There was selling and marrying in her eyes. At her age! He looked at the clouds and could not make up his mind which way to walk. More important: how was he to get out of that awful dinner tomorrow night?

COCKY
OLLY

At the end of term I often give a lift to two or three of my students who are going back to London. They talk; I listen. Halfway, about forty miles from the city, where the motorway rises and slices through the Downs, cutting one off from the towns that are merely names on the road signs, I interrupt their chatter to point out one or two prehistoric barrows. The youngsters listen politely. When we pass the sign, 'NEXT EXIT FORDHAMPTON', where a winding side road drops itself into the wooded country, I have the impulse to say that down there is a turning to Clapton St Luke, Fogham, and the Marshes – one of the paradises of my childhood – but I check it. And farther on we pass Newford, where I was at school when I was a girl, forty years ago. One of these days, when there is no one with me, I plan to go and look at these places, but I never do. The main road whips it all away.

I hear Newford is larger now; people commute from

there to London. Only a few used to take a train from Fordhampton, with its main street running down the hill to the small river, where we would lean from the bridge hoping to see the private trout in the pool where rich Londoners, one of them a Cabinet Minister, used to fish at weekends. On Monday mornings, when I was waiting at our station for the train to take me to school, the Cabinet Minister would be dressed in bowler hat, black coat, and striped trousers, and carrying his official case. Unlike the rest of the passengers, he would be trotting up to the end of the platform and back, often fifteen times: I counted. If my father drove me to the station he would give his big laugh and say loudly for anyone to hear, 'Bloody politician. Up to no good.' I was a weekly boarder at the school in Newford, and at first my mother drove me all the way and then would pick me up on Saturday mornings and drive me home to Upper Marsh, a different country, almost an island between the Downs, where the village people had a more drawling way of talking than the people in the towns. I had picked up the habit before my school days, from the children I played with on the farm near our house.

Marsh Hole really was like a deep hole, where four lanes met at a big farm. Our house was a mile up the road to Upper Marsh, a red mock-Tudor villa that I used to boast was Elizabethan. It was built between the wars. I also thought it was immense, but it was small. It looked out onto a large field of kale. At the back of our house (which my school friend Augusta called 'the eyesore') lay a two-mile stretch of water meadow that went to the foot of the bald Downs themselves. Rarely did one see anyone walking across it and not often any cattle grazing, either. The endless pampas (as I used to call it – one of my favourite words) was alive with insects in the spring and summer, and, from my bedroom, I used to feel I had only to stretch my finger to touch the prehistoric barrow at the top of the far-off hill and the curious chalk track that went in a zigzag scratch almost to the top. The water meadow began at a hedge at the bottom of our steep garden. I remember when I was thirteen gazing at it and feeling it all belonged to our family. This was because the people at Lower Marsh, half a mile farther down our lane, had exactly the same view, although we could not see their house even in the winter. A mound or tongue of coppice kept us from the sight of our nearest neighbours. Lower Marsh had a short avenue of elms leading to a farm where I used to play with the village boys. Lower Marsh House itself was large and grey, with big windows. The village boys said it was haunted. A strange tall man with a long black beard sometimes came out of it, and once I saw him in the road piddling into the hedge near our house. Another time, a funeral hearse went by and after that the black-bearded man did not appear again. But my mother told me I could not have seen all this, because I wasn't even born. Yet it is very vivid to me, and now I think I must have heard my parents talking of some such event much later.

But I know for a fact that years later Lower Marsh House was occupied by Major Short and his wife and a young boy, because I saw them hitting a shuttlecock in

the air once or twice as we drove past. Often at weekends if we were walking by we could see two or three
cars parked in the avenue of elms.

'Guests!' my mother would say.

'Weekend riffraff,' my father said. 'Gang of traitors.
Pacifists, long-haired pansies, atheists, bathing stark
naked in that swimming-pool. Friends of Hitler and
Stalin. Calls himself a major.'

'Well, he was,' my mother would say.

'First World War,' said my father, who was a brigadier.

'But, Buzzer,' my mother said – Buzzer was my
father's army nickname: they used to say he buzzed like
a wasp – 'didn't Major Short do rather well in that war,
got a medal and was badly wounded?'

'Got himself blown up, some fool dug him out.'

I always thought of the Major as a kind of fair-haired
elephant, with a huge chest, lying under tons of French
mud. My father had also been wounded. His left arm
creaked and he wore a black glove on his artificial hand.
He was a slight man with red hair and scalded patches
on his face and a high, sandy kind of voice with grit in
it, and when he talked of the Major he would get into
a temper. Then he'd laugh in the middle of it, and more
than once he added, 'Sends his boy to a god-awful
boarding school in Dorset run by pansies and refugees
wearing sandals, where the boys live in trees. Girls, too.
No wonder the little bastard runs away.'

'Surely not in trees, Buzzer,' my mother would say
in her high, thrilled, happy voice. I think that my mother
and father were thrilled by each other.

'Ruined by that nanny they had, too,' Father went
on. 'Not a lad I'd care to have in my command.'

These outbursts cheered my father. He was often up
and down to the War Office in London or away fishing.
At home he would either be ordering Mother's plants
about in the garden or sitting for hours playing patience
with his one hand. 'Crash, crash, tinkle, tinkle, tinkle,'
he would call out as he put a winning deal down. He
was thinking of glass flying about in French villages
when shells burst during that war.

Another thing that annoyed my father was that the
Shorts did not go to church. We were forbidden to know
them. Mother said it was nothing to do with that old
war. The real trouble was that our land almost joined
theirs and that the Major had cut down several fir trees
at the edge of it. My father, Mother said in her heavenly
voice, liked cover.

As for myself, I often thought about 'the little bastard'
Benedict, who not only lived in trees but was a 'run-away'
as well: that worried Mother, too. In spite of the quarrel
between the two men, I believed Mother and Mrs Short
sometimes met in Newford. They belonged to a musical
group, a quartet. More than once I saw the boy shopping
with his father and mother in Fordhampton, jumping up
and down with excitement as he called to them to look at
the posters of a gangster film at the cinema and talking
with a spluttering lisp. He had black hair like his mother's
and her same sunburned toasted skin – because he lived
in trees, perhaps – and he was handsome in his mother's
way. I used to wonder if he had run away that very day.
He was two years younger than I.

At fourteen, I was a studious girl. I longed to be a monitor at my school and I thought, as my father did, that Benedict was spoiled and that he ought to be 'taken in hand'. Often when I was out in our garden and looking at the Downs rising straight out of the marsh I was fascinated by the chalky track rising to the top and I would think of Benedict 'running' forty miles, at least, across country, and coming down that track as he came at last in sight of his home. I soon found out that in fact he did not run far. He had the nerve to telephone his father once he had escaped from that school of his and his father drove out at night, to pick him up outside some pub on the road. I was awed by this crime.

This and the thought of all those guests 'bathing naked' in the 'traitors'' house at Lower Marsh gripped me. In the holidays I would sometimes get through the hedge at the bottom of our garden and follow the rough ground until their house came into view and I would see the lawn of the Shorts' garden and keep an eye open for a sight of the runaway. Once, I thought I saw him with his mother walking across the water meadow picking wild flowers. Another time, he was coming in our direction and then drifted away. I used to think if he came near our garden I would shout out to him, 'What are you doing here? This is private property!' At last I decided to be illegal myself one weekend and to climb through our hedge and then walk cautiously all along the meadow till I could get a full view of the Shorts and their friends. Getting through the hedge always excited me. The air seemed freer on the other side, the smells different. I did this many times just for something to do, and at first went no nearer. I always took an apple with me, throwing it up and down as I walked, for I thought this would make the Shorts think I was passing by accident. Sometimes there was no one there, sometimes only Mrs Short digging in her garden. If it was a weekend there would be several men and women sitting in basket chairs on the long veranda or on the lawn. The lawn looked rough, but sometimes they played a mixture of bowls and croquet. In time I got bolder, passing within twenty yards of their garden. No sign of naked atheists or a swimming pool and only once a sight of Benedict, running from player to player. I heard the Major booming at him.

I gave up bothering about the Shorts. One hot and heavy afternoon at the end of that summer when the clouds hardly moved and the water meadow was as still as a photograph I got through our hedge again and walked across the water meadow, soon eating my apple, because I was thirsty. I looked at the St John's-wort, a yellow flower that swarms with disgusting caterpillars. The insects were biting and I kept brushing off the flies that were swirling round my head. I remember the swallows and crows were flying low. I was making for the wood at the bottom of the Downs and when I got there the wood pigeons had stopped cooing. Even the flies had gone. The wood had that cankered, damp smell – the smell of toadstools. It came into my head to see if there were any Red Blushers, which excited me, because there might be also what my fungus book called Poisonous or False Red Blushers – not that I would touch them but I liked to give myself a fright by staring at poisonous things and congratulating myself on knowing the difference. I didn't go too deeply into the wood but just shuffled through the dead leaves. The wood was darker, and presently I felt a big warm spit of rain on my face. Suddenly a shot went off, and I nearly jumped out of my skin and the silent wood pigeons came clattering out of the trees and went circling over the marsh. Then there was a long silence. I hurried out of the wood, and crackling sticks seemed to be coming after me. Suddenly the runaway came running out, carrying a gun. There were tears on his white face as he rushed at me.

'Quick! Quick!' he screeched. 'I've shot a bird. It's streaming with blood. It's frightful. It's still alive. It's flapping about.' And he grabbed hold of my arm.

I brushed back my hair. I heard myself saying in my father's voice, 'Stop waving that gun about. You can't leave a wounded bird.' I shook off his arm. 'Show me where it is,' I said.

'Up here! Up here!' he shouted out.

The bird was lying on the ground flapping one wing. There was blood on it and its white lids were closing upward. Benedict was afraid to touch it.

'It's got diphtheria,' he said. 'That's why I shot it.'

I knelt to pick it up.

'Birds don't get diphtheria,' I said.

'They *do*,' he screeched.

In a moment it was dead and horribly warm.

'We must bury it,' I said.

'No,' he said and stepped away. He was white and frantic.

'Come back,' I said. 'We can't leave it here. It's

cruel.' When I was small we always buried a bird if we found one dead.

'You must bury it,' I ordered. 'Dig a hole.' He had no knife. Nor had I. I told him to get a stick. He obeyed and we started digging a hole in the soft ground.

'Make it deep,' he said. He was excited now. At last the hole was deep enough and I put the poor bird in and raked the earth back. 'More leaves, more leaves,' he said. 'In case a stoat digs it up.'

'Did you get permission to have that gun?' I said. We were very hot about 'getting permission' for things at school.

'It's Glan's,' he said. Glanville was his father. 'Is this your half-term?'

'No,' I said. 'I'm a weekly boarder.'

'The Devil lives here,' he said. He had decided to frighten me.

'That's stupid,' I said. 'He doesn't exist.'

'It's a she-devil,' he said and he started jumping about in a jeering way.

'You're dotty,' I said.

I now felt several drops of rain, then it was pattering down. This stopped us talking and we looked up. There was a strange change of light and then a rumbling noise. The air was hot and heavy. Thunder! We hurried out of the wood, which was filled with a new sour smell, and just as we got out of the trees there was a long yellow flash of lightning. The peal of thunder came at once.

Benedict gave one of his shrill laughs. 'We'll be struck dead,' he screeched.

'We must get away from the trees,' I said. And then the rain came drenching down so that we could hardly see his distant house through it.

We started to run. My blue-and-white cotton dress was soaked at once, and we were nearly blinded by the rain. There was another flash as we stumbled through the humps of the meadow and then mud splashed our legs. We were running towards the Shorts' house; thank goodness my father was away fishing. We got across the ditch onto Benedict's forbidden lawn and ran up to the veranda of the house. I looked around as we ran: no swimming-pool in sight. The Major's wife was standing there calmly, and then the Major came out.

'Ah,' he said in a calm, insinuating, conspiratorial voice. 'The frightful Benedict and who has he brought with him? Is it the apple girl? I wonder. Yes, it is the apple girl.'

I realised I had been watched from the house every time I walked past. I was afraid of him.

'Oh, Benedict, you're drowned,' his mother said. 'What a bore you are. What on earth got into your head, when you know the Crowthers and the others are coming any minute. And look at poor dear Sarah. Get inside.' How did she know my name?

'Shall I take the firearm?' said Glanville Short to Benedict. 'I wonder how it came into your possession?'

All houses have their smell. The Shorts' house was larger than ours and smelled of thyme and oil paint and old wood fires.

We were taken up the plain polished stairs of the house – the stairs of *our* house were carpeted – passing

36

paintings of geometric faces which looked new. I remember two fat pink naked nymphs dancing on a big
seashell and two naked young men standing looking at
them. We passed a large room upstairs with bookcases
going up to the ceiling and a picture of that tall man
with the long black beard sitting in a basket chair and
stroking a cat. I was pushed into a bathroom.

'Get it all off, I think, don't you, Sarah, my dear?'
said Mrs Short, who had a book in her hand. 'While I
see to Benedict.'

What a bathroom! There was a blown-up painting or
photograph of an ancient ruin, which continued on three
walls of the room from floor to ceiling. I rubbed myself
with a towel. When Mrs Short came back I was staring
at the painting.

'Is that the Roman Forum?' I said, showing off.

'No, that is Persepolis, my dear. In Persia.' She
pointed to a figure on a grand but broken stairway.
'They say it is Darius – you remember? – but it doesn't
seem possible. Now, I don't know what we're going to
fit you out with.' She had brought a bundle of shorts
and jerseys with her.

'We were burying a dead bird,' I said.

'We could turn the legs up. Do you mind shorts?'

People coming, I thought, as I dried my hair. How
awful.

'Please don't bother,' I said as I pulled on the shorts.
'May I ring my mother?'

'Now you're a boy – what do you make of that?
Rather fun? How is your mother? I missed her at the
chamber music last week.'

So that rumour was true! I had always suspected that although we were ordered by my father not to know the Shorts, she and my mother still met at Newford.

'Rather chic, I think,' she said, looking at me. 'You must come down and get warm.'

We went along the corridor and round corners to a second flight of stairs, down to a kitchen and through a cloakroom with a telephone in it, and then across the hall into a large morning room, where there was a music stand with a sheet of music on it near a large window, and a violin propped against one wall. A radio was on a big table with books and newspapers and also on the same table there was a large, unfinished jigsaw puzzle spread out.

And that is how I remember Emma Short always: a small woman with small, brown brilliant eyes, as dark as Benedict was, wearing a plain but pretty dress, chattering and eagerly questioning herself as she stands before the large puzzle of some famous picture – a cathedral or a castle perhaps, with a river in the foreground. This one also had the figure of a man with a boat on the river. She is standing there picking up a piece and saying, 'How beastly they are to put so much water in these things. It's cheating. What a bore. Ah, now – here, do you think? No. No. Ah, perhaps here? You must look at the little wiggles.' And she put a curly piece of the puzzle into its place.

'You must know Mrs Figg,' she said.

'She teaches us French,' I said, surprised.

'I *know*!' said Mrs Short with a laugh. 'Too extraordinary. What do you make of her? Odd, do you find?

Her hats! Is Augusta a friend of yours? She's coming.'

Augusta Chambers, head girl of my school! Augusta – to see me dressed up like this!

I said again I must telephone to my mother to fetch me.

'Glan will do that,' she said. 'You must have some tea to warm you up.'

Through the window I saw two or three cars arrive. People and their children were soon jabbering in the hall. I heard Benedict screeching at them. As they came into the room Benedict was pulling Augusta's father by the wrist and saying, 'Foxey, Foxey, you're a murderer, a murderer. I'm going to report it to the police.'

'The number is 3052,' said Augusta's father. 'Shall I get it for you?'

There was a crowd of people taking off their coats in the hall. Benedict let Foxey's hand go, and Augusta came to me and said, 'What fun.' She whispered, 'Benedict is mad, as usual.'

I was muttering that I must go and getting nearer to the door to escape when Glanville Short stopped me. 'I have told your mother,' he said. 'You're staying to tea.'

Suddenly we were in a dining-room, sitting round a very large painted table, which seemed to be an astrological map.

'Your marvellous table,' said Augusta. And to me, 'Emma designed it. Isn't it wonderful?'

I was still embarrassed by my ridiculous clothes. I had never seen so many people in my life, all talking their heads off. At home we lived to ourselves, as my father said. Doors were always shut in our house. Here all the doors were open and names were flying about. Everyone was asking questions about other people. Benedict was screeching. The walls of the room were painted pale violet. A number of people I had never heard of were declared 'mad'. A Mary somebody was 'too extraordinary about her dogs'. There was news that someone called Stephanie had lost the manuscript of a novel she was writing, on a bus, for the second time.

'What do you make of Chester?' someone said.

The city or some person? I could not guess. I was out of my depth in this new language, but Benedict was listening eagerly, as if enchanted by mockery when his father spoke.

Augusta's handsome brother sat between me and Emma Short. He asked where I lived and went to school. When I told him about school, he said, 'Bad marks – it's on the Right Bank,' which amused him. It was a long time, almost a year, before I found out what he meant, and by then I was mad about him. People like the Shorts were sometimes called the Left Bank of an imaginary river like the Seine. Newford was very Right Bank, Fordhampton was very Left.

Suddenly tea was over. Emma Short groaned. 'It's still raining,' she said. 'What a bore. No croquet.'

'But Emma,' said Augusta's brother, 'we could take umbrellas.'

'Yes!' shouted Benedict, getting up. 'Umbrellas, umbrellas – we'll get umbrellas!'

'I think it will have to be Cocky Olly,' said Glan Short.

And they all shouted, 'Yes, Cocky Olly!'

'I don't know it,' I said.

'You do know it,' Benedict insisted. 'You must do. This is Cocky Olly Lane – everyone plays it. It's Prisoner's Base.'

'Cocky Olly' is the name that jumps into my mind even now when I drive past the signpost to Fordhampton. And when I look back on it who could have been more of a Cocky Olly than myself, chasing the runaway boy across the fields.

'Cocky Olly!' we all shouted.

'No one to go into the bedrooms,' said Emma Short. 'Library and bathrooms are free.'

'Including, I hope,' said Foxey, 'the pig's bathroom.' He meant that Glanville had kept half a pig in brine in one of the bathrooms during the war. I had heard of this at home, and I had been told that it was illegal to cure a pig without registering the fact with the agricultural inspector. My father always said Major Short ought to be reported to the inspector and sent to jail.

And so with Foxey as Cocky Olly to start us off, the grown-ups and we children raced up the stairs and hid all over the house. Soon we were shouting warning cries of 'Cocky Olly on the back stairs!' as everyone raced away. 'Cocky Olly in the library!' 'Cocky Olly in the passage!' 'Cocky Olly in Annie's room!' and we raced up another flight, and Augusta, who had been caught, was shouting, 'Rescue, rescue!' and Benedict was crying for rescue, too. I got to him and touched him. He was free. He was the most excited of us all. Round the house, up and down, we went. On a desk in the library, where Glanville worked, I came upon a huge book called *The Building of the Pyramids*. It was written, Augusta told me, by that old man with the long black beard – the one I had seen peeing into the hedge, whose portrait was on the wall, not easy to see because the afternoon was dark. The rain was still coming down. Then the hue and cry came again, the sound of scattering people. I ran along the passage and made for a door where the passage turned a corner. Benedict had scooted there. We collided and stepped back into a small room where the curtains were drawn. Suddenly Benedict locked the door. 'That's not fair,' I said. I can hear myself, even now, saying it.

Benedict said in his shrill voice, 'There's a dead body in here.'

I was not going to be scared by him. I remembered what Foxey had done when Benedict called him a murderer.

'Yes,' I said. 'I know. I've reported it. It's on the floor. Give me the key or I'll put the light on.'

He gave me the key at once.

'This is your room,' I said.

'It isn't,' he said. 'It used to be Nanny's, but we threw her out.' I told him he couldn't scare me, and, in fact, after that I couldn't get rid of him. He followed me everywhere as we chased round in the game.

The grown-ups had gone down to the drawing room and eventually, hot and puffed, we went in to join them. It was a greenish silky room. Glanville was handing out orange juice to cool us down, and small glasses of gin, I suppose, to the grown-ups and to Augusta's brother, too. Glanville moved slowly, politely, with a sly conspiring look in his eyes as he gave us our drinks. He had been in the middle of telling a story when we rushed in, and now he continued. He had been on a jury at Winchester, he said, and there was evidence from a policeman who said he had seen the prisoner signalling to a confederate on a racecourse, and then the judge had said, 'A signal, officer? Would you be kind enough to do the signal for us?' and the officer made strange movements with his hand. The judge said, 'Officer, would you mind doing that again?'

Glanville had a gift for acting. He could make you feel guilty by rolling his eyes and looking mysterious. In a fish shop in Fordhampton when I was with my mother we once heard him saying in his quiet accusing voice to the fishmonger, 'Have you *fish*?'

I looked round at the pictures on the walls of the drawing room. There were two clowns and there was a painting of a sculptured head of a girl in profile, mounted on a short marble stand, a girl with large eyes, very beautiful.

'It's a Stolz,' Augusta whispered to me.

'No, it isn't,' said her brother. 'It's a Webb in her Stolz period.' And to me he said, in Mrs Short's manner, 'What do you make of it?'

'It looks chopped off,' I said. I saw Augusta's brother was disappointed in me.

I looked at the heads of all the people in the room. They seemed to be like people from another planet. I was in love with them all and did not want to leave.

And then Foxey said, 'We must go,' and Augusta said to me, 'We'll drop you.'

'No, I'll walk. It's only up the lane.'

'You must come again,' said Mrs Short.

'I wonder whether we shall see more of the apple girl,' said Glan in his conspiring mocking tone. 'I think we shall.'

I remember sitting next to Augusta's brother in the back of the car and Benedict waving frantically to us.

'Where are your clothes?' my mother asked when I was dropped at our house.

I had forgotten them.

'What a sight you look.'

I could not stop talking about everything and everyone I had seen – the house, the huge tea table, the puzzle on Mrs Short's table, the Persepolis in the bathroom. I explained that it was not my fault I had gone there, but I was worried about what my father would say. Mother made light of it. All she wanted to know was whether Benedict had played his violin.

This startled me.

'He is going to be *good*,' my mother said in her thrilled voice. She was astonished that I did not know.

I could not go to sleep for thinking about it all: the rooms, the stairs, the girl's head, Benedict locking me in the room, and Augusta's brother. I looked at my room and hated our furniture and the smell of polish, and wanted to run away.

It was only in the morning that I remembered I had not seen the swimming-pool.

I admit that I left my wet clothes behind so that I would be able to return. The following morning, I went back to Lower Marsh openly by the road and down the avenue of elms, with a bundle of the Shorts' clothes under my arm, but kept back the shirt until it could be washed. The air was fresher after the storm. The front door of the house was open. There was no bell or knocker. I could hear Glanville talking on the telephone, which perhaps for some secret reason was in the cloakroom. At our house we had a proper telephone fitted in our hall.

I heard Glanville say on the telephone, 'So you think well of Gentle Annie do you? I had rather fancied –' and I think he said 'Monte Cristo'. And then, 'Rather dangerous, do you think? The going will be heavy after all the rain. Well, we must hope.' Then he must have changed the subject, for in a conspiring, private voice he was saying, 'I am inclined to agree with you, Foxey. I fancy that Oedipus is coming into the open. He is digging a grave in the garden – indeed, *two* graves. But we don't despair, Foxey. There is a filly, and we're pinning our hopes there. We shall have to see how it goes. Goodbye, Foxey.'

Now what was that about?

Then he came out of the cloakroom and saw me.

'Ah, what have we here? The apple girl without her apple. She has brought a parcel. What can that be?'

He took the parcel and then, in his plotting way, said, 'We must discover where the frightful Benedict is. Do you think he may be in the garden? Shall we go and see?'

I had decided that when he was buried under tons of earth by a land mine, or whatever it was, in the First World War, Glanville must have saved his life by asking himself innumerable questions. Perhaps that is silly, but he always looked at me or anyone else so steadily as he spoke that he was outside time and his blue eyes cast a spell. This made me shy, because he was not an old man. Now he led me through the house onto the long veranda and we looked down across the lawn. No sign of Benedict, so we went round the side of the house and there, in the paddock, we saw him. He was digging with difficulty in the tufty grass, and when we got to him we saw he had taped out two long rectangles side by side and had dug a few spadefuls of earth out of the end of one. As we watched, Benedict stuck the garden fork into the ground and danced around it.

'Can he be looking for buried treasure?' the Major asked.

Benedict jumped about crying, 'Guess, guess, guess. Don't tell her, Glan.'

I said he was making a flowerbed.

'No, no, no,' he called out. 'Guess.'

Mrs Short came up from the garden and the Major explained why I was there. Benedict was annoyed because we were not talking to him.

'He says it is a swimming-pool – one for men, one for ladies,' said Mrs Short.

We all laughed.

Benedict looked from one to the other of us. 'I have changed it,' he said. 'It's an Egyptian tomb for Pharaoh.'

'And this one, perhaps, for his wife?' said the Major, pointing to the second rectangle.

'Where is the pyramid?' I said.

'It's going to be a barrow,' said Benedict. 'An ancient mound.'

The Major and his wife strolled away, and Benedict and I were left alone. I picked up the garden fork and tried to dig. 'Don't do that,' he said, and pulled the fork from me, rather frightened. 'It's boring,' he said.

It was a lazy morning, one of those long mornings – how long they are when one is young – when you wander about and every minute is as long as an hour.

'I'm going to see the dead bird,' he said at last.

I did not want to go home. I thought, This is where I want to stay, so I followed him. We crossed the hedge into the water meadow, where the air was cool, and listened to the swish of our shoes against the wiry grass and watched the insects jump away and stopped to listen to the larks singing like electric bells high up in the sky and tried to see them, and we seemed to walk from one electric bell to another. Like Benedict I was playing at running away. First he went ahead fast, but I soon caught up and passed him.

'Beat you,' I said, and rumpled his head as I passed. He began to chase me. We passed the end of the wood where the dead bird was and got across the stream, where we messed about with sticks in the water and startled birds. Then we began to climb. I wanted to get to the top of the barrow, but it was longer and higher than I had imagined it would be. The view grew wider and wider and went on for miles, and there was no sound now. We were high above the singing larks. I could see our house and Benedict's standing quiet with the sun on them. We stopped and sat down. We were sitting on the bones of people who had died *millions* of years ago. There was no sound here except the wind, but then we heard the baaing of a ram. It sounded to me like the voice of a buried man, but I did not say this. We got up from where we were sitting and looked for it but could see nothing. The sound must have come from the ram far below. I nearly said, 'The heights! How I love them!' but I didn't. Benedict, I thought, is too young; I was centuries older than he was. I wanted to stay there for ever – not with Benedict but, say, with Augusta's brother, and when we stood for a last look on the miles of flat fields and clumps of trees where there would be a church tower and little houses on the far side, with a road wriggling round a wood, I wanted to go there, too. Suddenly – I don't know why – thinking of Augusta's brother, I marched up to Benedict and kissed him and ran off. He didn't like this and picked up a thorny stick and chased after me.

I stopped. 'Why do you run away from school?' I asked severely.

'I hate it,' he said at once. 'It's boring. I'm not going back.'

The Devil was there, he went on. Benedict and the Devil! The Devil was dressed in red, he said. This time the Devil was the man who taught music there at his school. He was ignorant, stupid.

It was getting late. We went stumbling down the steep

path, and as we got lower I could hear the skylarks again, no higher than my shoulder but far out over the fields below. I could almost have caught one of them.

When we got down to the meadow Benedict was angry when I said I had to get back home. 'Stay, stay,' he said, 'I'll let you dig.' But I said no, I didn't want to dig. He followed me across the meadow to our hedge, still saying 'Stay.' I said I had to pack up and go back to school in the afternoon. When I got through the hedge and called out 'Goodbye,' he shouted 'I hate you!' I saw him walking away and then suddenly he ran and then he was out of sight. I don't know why I kissed him when we were on the barrow.

Everything changed at my school in Newford after that party at Lower Marsh. Augusta, who was a good deal older than I and taller, had never taken much notice of me, but now she came floating round me like a swan. She had long golden hair and large grey dreaming eyes that narrowed and dwelled on you in an inspecting way. She said, 'I didn't know you knew the Shorts,' in a way that suggested I had hidden a secret from her. Her voice seemed to float on romantic secrets. She was also our chief mimic and gossip. She'd do Mrs Figg's sarcastic voice, and she knew which teacher was in love with an old don at Oxford who was married. She called two girls who doted on the art master 'Picasso's Doves', and the headmistress 'the blessed St Agnes'. To be with her was like reading a novel in serial parts; she paused and we knew there were chapters to come.

I told her that we did not really know the Shorts,

though my mother, I thought, often met Mrs Short at a musical quartet at Newford.

She narrowed her questioning eyes. 'I adore Glan and Emma, don't you?'

And before I knew what I was saying I said there was some trouble about fir trees.

'Fir trees!' said Augusta with a laugh that egged me to go on, but I had come to a lame end.

We were going into supper and Mrs Figg passed us. 'Don't dawdle, Sarah,' she said.

I was not a dawdling girl, and I saw that I must have been copying Augusta's dawdling walk. It was new to me, and I felt I had grown up several months. As we separated and went to our different tables Augusta said, off-hand, 'Of course, Benedict's quite mad. My father says it goes back to that awful pious nurse he had. She used to tell him that the Devil would get him and that he would go to hell. And then there was that awful Webb business.' And, with that, she glided away.

But the phrase 'that awful Webb business' and Augusta walking away with her I-know-more-than-you-do look made me dog Augusta whenever I could. And I could see by her face that she noticed this. We went off the next day to play tennis on the school court. She was a slapdash tennis player, and even the few balls that came over the net seemed to know something. When we left the court and went to our dormitory to change I said, 'My father didn't cut down those fir trees. It was old Webby who used to work for the Shorts as well as for us.'

Augusta stood there with her blouse off. Her grown-

up breasts, larger than mine, seemed to be staring at
me. The bell rang and we hadn't washed.

'Run along,' she said. 'Actually,' she said – we all
said 'actually' in a cutting way in those days – 'I was
talking about Glanville's first wife. She died years ago.
She drowned.'

I felt I was like some silly fish dangling on a hook in
hot air. I could not breathe.

'Come along, girls,' Mrs Figg called from the door of
the dormitory. I choked my way into my clothes. I
sluiced my face and through the water I saw the astonish-
ing stone face of the drowning Webb in the drawing
room at Lower Marsh.

Poor Benedict, I thought, and I ran down the clattering stairs to the dining room. I mumbled my way through
grace and saw Augusta across the room saying grace
beautifully, her lovely chin raised. Later she ate slowly,
while I was racing through my food and spilled my milk.
I was still wriggling on Augusta's hook. I was in her
power.

But Augusta was merciful to me, or else, I suppose,
she saw the kind of opportunity she loved. If she was
dreamy, she was also crisp.

In our free time it was easy for girls to be in twos,
lying in the grass, and at last I was able to say, 'Poor
Benedict, his mother drowned.' This explained the
strange things he did, and his talk of the body in the
room.

'I did not say that,' said Augusta scornfully. 'Emma
is his mother. Glan was married to Webb. *Then* he
married Emma. What a thing to say! Did your father

say that? If he did, it's very wicked,' she said sharply.

I said no, he'd never said anything like that, nor my mother, I swore. Augusta was still suspicious of this, but at last she saw how confused I was, and she forgave me. She said that Glanville had married a Miss Webb when he came home after the First World War; everyone was mad about her. It was not until much later that I began to wonder how Augusta knew the story. It must have happened *before* the war and she wasn't born then. But she said that Webb had gone off to Egypt with a painter called Stolz and that he had left her, and so she had come home and drowned herself in the river at Fordhampton.

The one where father can't afford to fish, I thought. And then I thought of Benedict digging a grave for Pharaoh and his wife in his garden.

I had already told Augusta about this the day after Cocky Olly, but when I mentioned it again now, Augusta cut the story short. 'That boy is always digging,' she said. 'He wants to be an archaeologist, like that man in Glanville's library.' And she said dreamily, 'I would never be a second wife, unless he was like Glanville.'

We got up from the grass laughing. I mean, *I* laughed; Augusta didn't. Anyway, she said, Emma and Glan were sending Benedict to the grammar school in Newford. That would stop him running away because he'd come home every day by train. And she gave me one of her narrow-eyed looks. The Shorts were her possession.

The long holidays began. My father took us to Devonshire to stay in a hotel near a place where he went fishing. Mother and I went on long walks, and the only event of the day was to come back by the bridge over the river to catch sight of him. We were not allowed to go near him when he was fishing. Once or twice we drove ten miles to a high red-faced cliff – they were not chalky cliffs as they are in our part of the country. The waves were forever staining the sand red near the shore. We used to park on the cliff with other cars and walk not too near the edge and look at the sea glittering some days and on others tumbling fast down the Channel. I loved the Channel because it was wider here. This was the only time I thought of the Shorts and Benedict, for they were in Brittany. *La mer*: what a beautiful word! We had a set book by Pierre Loti to read in the holidays. My mother said she, too, had had to read it at school when she was a girl, yet she was no help with the words I didn't know.

So, back home again. It seemed dull. I rushed to my post at the end of our garden and looked across the water meadow, but there was no sight of Benedict on the first day. In the middle of the week I did see him in the distance with a girl taller than he and making for his house. I waved. They did not see me, and I tried to make myself look larger when they came into closer view. I waved again. They still did not see me. I felt something like a red-hot electric wire run through me – a wire that seemed to turn into a flame, as if I were alight. Then I went icy cold. Benedict was with Augusta! I was flaming with jealousy. I watched till they went out of sight.

My father was in the garden talking to my mother,

who was pulling up weeds. I got carried away and went out to the road and walked along to the Shorts' drive. There were cars outside the house, one of them Foxey's red car. A party. And I wasn't invited. I was stiff with misery. I went back to my room and tried to read, but I was listening, for hours it seemed to me, to hear the cars drive away. When I went to bed my jealousy went. I remembered that the next week I would see Benedict on the train to and from school.

But at first this was not so. On the first day of term Augusta told me that Benedict's mother was going to drive him to his grammar school and bring him back each day. So I became a parcel again on my weekly journey. On Monday mornings I saw the politician doing his morning trot up and down the platform, and weekend people going to London with their papers, and a few grammar-school boys who got in at King's Mill and played cards all the way. Their school caps had a yellow ring round them. On Saturday afternoons there was always a large crowd of them going back to their homes in King's Mill or Fordhampton. About a dozen of them would stand on the platform bashing one another with their cases, and cheeking the woman who ran the buffet. Sometimes she turned them out. They crowded round the slot machines and tried to force them to yield up coins. I used to sit on a seat watching them. The porters grinned at the boys, but the ticket inspector hated the way they pushed past him. Sometimes a boy would be pushed onto my seat and I would walk away higher up the platform. There was a fat boy who was always eating chocolate.

The first Saturday I saw Benedict on the platform, he was keeping clear of the other boys. 'Hullo,' he said eagerly in his high voice, and the fat boy mocked, 'Squeaky's got a little t-tart.'

They stared at us and then went on pushing one another around. Benedict was carrying his violin case. I had never seen that before. I asked him why he wasn't wearing the school cap.

'Because I hate it,' he said.

I can't remember what we talked about except that I told him that I had seen him with an old lady walking across the water meadow and had waved to him. He was startled.

'A witch,' he said.

'No, it wasn't,' I said. 'It was Augusta. Don't tell her I said that.'

'I'll tell,' he said.

I knew he would, because every now and then after our train came in and we took our seats he said, 'I'll tell, I'll tell.'

At Fordhampton, Glan was waiting for him, and my mother was there as well.

'Aha!' said Glanville in his insinuating way. 'The apple girl.'

'It seems damn silly,' said my father to my mother when I got home. 'Why couldn't he have given Sarah a lift and saved you the trouble? Save petrol, too. Typical socialist.'

'You don't give the boy a lift,' Mother said.

'Don't be an owl,' Father said. 'That man's got nothing to do.'

So every Monday and Saturday I travelled on the train with Benedict. He had become quieter and it seemed that he had settled into the school. It was 'beastly' there, of course, but chiefly, he said, because the music master was angry when he told him the school piano was out of tune. He also hated Prayers, and the fat boy who got into the train at King's Mill was the Devil. This came out one morning when a man across from us was reading a newspaper with a headline in big print: 'CLIFF MURDER: HUNT FOR BRIGHTON YOUTH.' Benedict began jumping up and down in his seat and said the fat boy had done it. 'It's Fatty! It's Fatty!' he said in a furious whisper. I told him not to be silly. At school I told Augusta this was now the only sign of Benedict's being mad, but she had changed this term. She said it was Glanville who put these ideas into his son's head. Foxey said so, too. But after this Benedict was calm. One day he brought his stamp collection and he showed it to me, and once I ruffled his black hair when he said I was as fat as Augusta. I knew what he meant: I was growing up. I told him Augusta would marry him if he was not careful, and I laughed because he looked scared. He was very polite after that.

I enjoyed those train rides and I missed him for two weeks when he had flu. I was glad to see him when he reappeared on the platform at Newford Station. I had got there late because I had gone into one of the shops in the town to buy a lipstick like Augusta's. I had run all the way from the shop, frightened that I had missed the train. At first I didn't see Benedict. Some boys were crowded round the fat boy as usual, begging him to give them a bit of his chocolate. The fat boy was backing away from them and Benedict was watching. The fat boy was sly and stood back against the wall, looking around for some way of escape. One boy was pulling at his arm. Suddenly the fat boy broke from them and went up to Benedict, snatched his cap from his pocket, and cried, 'Put your cap on, Squeaky, or I'll report you.'

Benedict stood holding his violin case and did not put his cap on, and the fat boy suddenly stepped forward and pulled the cap down over Benedict's eyes and face. I called out, 'Leave him alone.'

And then I saw Benedict do a stupid thing. He pulled his cap off and sent it flying off the platform and onto the railway track, and then, white with fright, he dashed at the fat boy and struck him on the shoulder with his violin case, screeching out, 'I'll kill you!'

The fat boy moved away, frightened. Two women were watching us, and one of them said, 'I will report you to your headmaster,' and she said to her friend, 'It's Major Short's boy.' I got Benedict by the sleeve and we walked away from the crowd. I was giddy with temper and walked him far up the platform, and when I looked back I saw the boys gaping at the cap lying on the railway line. Two boys were beginning to follow us, but the others were still crowding round Fatty. And then the train came in. I got Benedict into a first-class carriage in front. Three of Fatty's crowd raced up looking for us, but I pulled down the blind. I could hear the porters bawling, and the boys ran back. We sat still; the compartment had a notice saying 'Ladies Only'. There was a long wait and a strange silence at our end of the train. I let down the window and saw some of the boys getting off the train, all laughing. I heard a porter shout, 'Not this train!' A whistle blew. The train, I saw, was much longer than the train we usually took.

'We're on the wrong train,' I said. 'It's the express. Quick. It doesn't stop at Fordhampton,' and I tried to open the door. Then the train – one of the new diesels – moved out fast. I turned round. Benedict was lounging back on the seat.

'I knew!' he said, laughing at me.

'You beast,' I said.

I was scared. I saw the last of the pink houses of Newford and heard the chime of the signal box, as final and frightening as if it were killing itself with laughter. My father and mother would be waiting for me at Fordhampton and the train would whiz through. And that woman from Lower Marsh who had heard me shout in the mixup with the boys – she would report it all to my father. I lost my head.

'Why didn't you tell me it was the wrong train?' I said. 'I hate you.'

'I'm running away,' he said, delighted by my terror. 'I hate that school. I hate Glanville. I'm not going back.'

There is a long wooded stretch outside Newford and all the leaves on the trees seemed to be talking about us. Had he planned it?

'Where are you going?' I said.

He was sitting there gloating and grinning. 'To London,' he said.

'But that's in the opposite direction. This train goes to Bath.'

'I'll get a London train there,' he said.

'You're mad. It's hundreds of miles away.'

What frightened me was that I had only two shillings on me.

'How much money have you got?' I said.

'My aunt lives in Bath. She'll give me the money,' he said.

The train was speeding. Two little stations went by like a shout.

'The Devil is on this train,' he said with glee. 'I saw him on the platform.'

I was standing up still, and the train swerved at King's Mill when it crossed the river. A man was fishing there. I fell onto my seat. I was tired of Benedict and his Devil.

'I'll rape you,' he said.

'You won't,' I said. 'Silly little Squeaky.' And I got up and rumpled his hair. 'You'd better look at your violin. You smashed it when you hit that boy.'

This stopped him. He opened his case and took out his violin and looked at it very carefully and then he took up his bow and played one or two notes. They sounded very sad. All this time I had been trying not to cry, and it was the sound of those notes, like someone speaking, that stopped me. In that moment I recovered my wits. I looked about the compartment and noticed the communication cord. A notice said 'Emergency. To Stop Train Pull the Cord. Penalty for Improper Use £5.' I was scared. When the train got near Fordhampton I knew I was going to pull the cord and make it stop there. I sat down and got out one of my school books and pretended to read, but I was looking at the fields. When the train got to Flour Mill I would get ready to pull the cord. This calmed me. I got up and said, 'I am going to the lavatory.' I was dying to go. 'There's one for you at the other end of the corridor,' he said.

There was the door marked 'Toilet Vacant'. I went in. The window was of frosted glass so that I couldn't see out, but I could tell by the sound of the train crossing the river where we were. We'd crossed one bridge. There were two more to come. I knew how long that took. I wasn't long in the lavatory before someone tried the door. I waited. Then I pulled the catch. It had stuck. It wouldn't open at first; when it did there was the ticket inspector on the other side. The inspector always tested the door in order to catch any one hiding from him. He was a big man with a red face and a black moustache like a wet paintbrush.

'Sorry, Miss. Ticket, please.'

'It's in my bag in the compartment,' I said. He looked at my hat – we wore straw hats with a red band at my school – and slowly followed me to the compartment. Benedict was not there, and as I opened my bag I heard a deep rumbling noise, louder than the noise of river bridges. We were rushing over the High Street at Fordhampton. The station platform screeched at us, people flew away in a stream of dots, the green top of the town hall danced away, and the brick orphanage on the outskirts of the town looked down on us from fifty narrow windows. I had forgotten this was an express train. With a final clap Fordhampton vanished, the points clattered, and the oak woods closed in on us. Benedict came into the compartment.

'Ticket,' the ticket inspector said to Benedict, who got out his train pass.

'We're going to Bath,' Benedict said coolly.

'You're in first class!' said the inspector. 'Ford-hampton, it says here. That your violin? We've passed Fordhampton.'

He took my train pass and looked at it and said the same thing. Then he sat down with us and got out a printed pad. 'Both going to Bath? Plenty of room in third class in the next coach.'

He slowly turned the pages of his pad. 'You'll be owing me some money,' he said. 'Ten pounds each. You got in at Newford, I see. It comes expensive.' He looked very sly when he said this and then sighed and said sharply, 'First class – let me see. Fifteen pounds each, I make it. Holidays begun early, eh? Playing in a concert?' He was looking around in the compartment, and I knew he was trying to see if we had smashed the lightbulbs or slashed the seat.

'We got into the wrong train and some boys locked us in. We thought it was the Fordhampton train,' I said. 'My father is waiting for us. He's a brigadier. It's terrible. No one told us at Newford. I'm not going to Bath, and we missed our lunch.'

'Well, it will be a long wait,' said the inspector. 'But your friend's going to Bath. With his violin?'

'No, I'm going to London. I'm in the school orches-tra,' Benedict said calmly.

I was so amazed I could only say, 'Benedict!'

'I am,' said Benedict.

'It's a funny way to go to London. Down to Bath, up to London, wrong way round. Cost you more. Twenty-five pounds, I make it.'

'Where is the buffet car?' said Benedict, putting on an important voice.

The inspector said it was two coaches back. 'Stay where you are,' he said. He got up slowly. He put his pad in his pocket and said he'd be back later on. We waited and waited.

'Why did you tell such lies? We'll be arrested.'

'Let's go to the buffet car,' Benedict said. 'I'm hungry.'

If only I hadn't bought that lipstick. With only my two shillings, we couldn't pay for lunch.

The train broke out of the Downs, where there was a white horse carved on the hill, and into unknown country, herds of cows in the fields, farms, chickens, horses galloping away. This flat country went on, mile after mile. Farther and farther. I worried where we would go in Bath, where we would sleep the night. Terrible tales came into my mind of girls attacked on trains. I was thinking about what my father had said about the Shorts.

'You're not giving a concert,' I said. 'You can't even play.'

'I can,' he said. He opened his case and got his violin out, but I asked if he had got any money. He pulled out a few coppers from his pocket. 'Come on,' he said. 'Let's go to the buffet car. I'll tell them to send the bill.'

But before we could move the inspector came back

with a young man who stood in the doorway studying us and murmured something I couldn't catch.

'Stand up, Ben,' this man said.

'My name is Benedict,' said Benedict. He could be as cool and ironical as Glanville.

The young man said, annoyed, 'Where's your school cap?'

I burst out, 'A boy threw it on the line at Newford when the train was coming in.'

'What was his name?' asked the man.

'Fatty,' said Benedict.

'Better check at Castle Wadney,' said the young man to the inspector. They went off down the corridor.

The train was gliding past wide fields of mustard, a few big clouds were hanging still in the sky. Presently the train slowed down almost to a standstill, and when I looked out I saw a gang of men standing back: they were working on the line. I can still remember every one of their faces looking up at me. Then we crawled past watercress beds to Castle Wadney, a town on a hill but with no castle that I could see. The train had stopped.

'Police,' whispered Benedict excitedly.

The inspector came back and said, 'Soon get you back, Miss. You're getting out here.'

At that busy station porters were rolling milk cans down the platform. We were taken to the station-master's office, a dark room smelling of ink and tea. The stationmaster was drinking a cup in between talking on the telephone, and there was a machine somewhere that clicked dot, dot, dash. A man at another table called

'Brighton on the line for you' to a very clean young man with hair short at the neck, who went to the telephone.

One of these new men looked at our train passes and asked our names again. I showed him mine on my exercise book. Someone was having a row with the stationmaster, who held the phone away from his ear.

'Sure it's not Knowles?' the smooth young man asked Benedict.

'Short. Short. Short,' Benedict jeered.

'Short,' I joined in. 'I mean he's Short, I'm –'

'I'm asking him,' said the smooth young man. 'How do I know your name's Short, son?' he asked.

And then Benedict did a thing I'll never forget. He turned his back to the man and pulled the neck of his jacket clear of his neck until the name tape was showing.

The detective held the jacket and called to the two new men. 'Take a dekko at this.'

'"Short",' they both said. 'OK, Sonny.'

'Hold on, they're on the line,' said the stationmaster into the telephone. Then he beckoned to us.

Glanville was on the line. Emma, too. And my father. When we had stopped talking to them the two inspectors had gone and so had our train. We were going to be sent back on the 3.44.

One of the detectives said, 'Sorry, Miss.' And the other said, 'On the lookout for a lad from Brighton. You won't miss your concert,' he said to Benedict and went off.

'Watch out,' whispered Benedict. 'They'll follow us.' He was delighted.

The stationmaster took us to the buffet and told the

woman there to give us what we asked for and to give the bill to him. He told Benedict his daughter was taking piano lessons. We were put on the 3.44 to Fordhampton, and I felt sad going back.

'It was the Brighton Cliff Murder,' said Benedict. 'They thought we were in on it.'

And indeed a youth had taken the hand brake off his parents' car, jumped out, and left them to go over the cliff. There was a picture of a boy very like Benedict with curly hair. We saw it all when a man got in at one of the stops with the picture on the inside page and a headline saying 'HUNT MOVES TO WEST COUNTRY'. I muttered to Benedict, 'Keep quiet or I'll strangle you.'

Benedict started bouncing with delight on his seat. He said that Glan had told him all about the murder. And he started to tell me. The Devil would be in it, I knew.

'*Stop it*,' I said. 'Not now. You promised me.'

The train was a slow one. The man got out at Stockney. And then I said, 'Why did you say you were going to Bath?'

'To see the Roman ruins,' he said.

'But you said London, too, to give a concert,' I said. I couldn't keep up with him.

'I am going to the College of Music next term,' he said.

I began to tease him. 'There was a devil on *this* train – it was you,' I said and gave him a push.

There is nothing to say about our arrival at Fordhampton, except that my mother was talking to Mrs Short, and Benedict was talking all the time to Glan, telling him how he had shown his name tape to the detective. Father was talking to the stationmaster, who was shaking his head.

'I gave the stationmaster at Newford a blowing up,' Father said. 'I mean, suppose they'd been troops?'

'It's the staff, you know what I mean,' said the stationmaster. 'Your daughter's here.'

'Oh,' said my father, astonished to see me. And then he saw Glanville and stiffened. 'All present and correct,' he said sarcastically.

In the car driving home I began telling my father and mother what had happened, but Father said, 'Wait till we get home.'

Mother said, 'You should have pulled the alarm cord.'

Father said, 'Costs five pounds. I haven't got five pounds.'

I didn't say anything about Benedict's saying he was running away. Father was already revelling in the war he was now beginning with the railway company. He was going to write to the chairman at once. He was going to get someone at the War Office to blow them up. Mother's eyes shone.

When I went to school on Monday Benedict was not on the train, but Mrs Figg had heard the story, because Mother had rung the school. Augusta knew, too. Then she told me that once a man had exposed himself in a train when she was there, in a full compartment!

What did she do? 'Nothing,' she said grandly. 'I turned my head away and looked out of the window.'

That weekend my mother picked me up at my school and Benedict at his and drove us back to the Shorts, and I was invited for tea. Father said it was the least they could do.

Mrs Short was standing by her puzzle when I got there, a new one of a castle.

'It's a beast,' she said. There were a dozen people at that beautiful table and Benedict was crowing and interrupting his father. Then it was Cocky Olly again and all of us racing around.

A TRIP
TO THE
SEASIDE

After she had dropped her sister off at the hotel Sarah drove *Mr* Andrews (as she pointedly called him) along the sea front to the station. They were stiffened by silence. He got out and said coldly, 'Thank you. Goodbye,' but she got out too and said, 'Oh, no. I'm coming on to the platform to see you on to the train.' He looked at his watch: for seven minutes he would have to put up with her. She even stood close to him; until the London train came she was not going to let him out of her sight. Even when, to escape, he excused himself and went to the door marked 'Gentlemen' she marched with him and stood outside, vigilant. When he came out and the train arrived at last she almost pushed him into the nearest compartment, and would have closed the door but other passengers were crowding after him. Still she did not move, and at the open door she started muttering short sentences. She said: 'We don't want you down here messing up her life again and trading on her feelings.'

Andrews did not speak. He sat in his corner seat, his face as pink as Aberdeen granite, looking straight ahead of him, ignoring her, his chin raised, his nose on its dignity. She was a short and avid woman with dry grey hair and about his age. Just before the door was closed by a porter and the train gave a starting jolt she shouted: 'I hope we never set eyes on you again.'

Some passengers raised their newspapers after a glance at him. Others stared. In the first five minutes as the train picked up speed he sat without changing his expression. Then he got up and left the compartment with a look of contempt for everyone there and, checking his ticket, made for an empty compartment in the first-class coach. There he was alone, looking blankly at the villas, trees and fields wheeling back in the watery spring dusk.

That morning Andrews had arrived from London just to spend the day, even possibly a week if things went well. You could never tell. Anyway there would be a sniff of sea air to clean his kippered London lungs. He thought of fish as he walked from the station, had lunch at a hotel called the George, which seemed to be the best place, fancied oysters, a Dover sole, a glass of white wine, which brought out that pink in his face. Then, better dressed than the Easter crowd, he went for an inspecting stroll. He was a widower of sixty-five who had spent his business life in the carpet trade. It had struck him as a good omen and a compliment to his gifts as a salesman that the lounge of the hotel had a new chocolate-coloured carpet with a design of huge chrysanthemums on it – one of his 'lines', the Demeter

Floral. It wore well. He had indeed the muted walk of a man for whom the streets were carpeted and the smile of a public benefactor with a quiet surprise in his pocket. He was looking for a wife. He looked at one or two houses that were for sale, for a house was what he wanted: a house by the sea. The prices were very high: the dream had to go. He turned off to the address of Miss Louisa Browder, who had been his secretary for years before his job had come to a sudden end. As he came up in the train he had thought of her as a possibility, if also a *faute de mieux.*

To call on Louisa Browder would require nerve, for she had walked out of his office after a row five years before, but he was not a man to entangle himself in the rights and wrongs of the past. He knew the trouble had started at a trade exhibition in Brighton – a much larger resort than this – and he put it down to her age, or perhaps her mother's death, to those family things like the bother with her jealous sister who had never liked him – things that upset women and make them take it out on others, just as his wife Daisy used to do. In *her* jealous way – jealousy her only fault – she would shout 'Louisa's a woman and don't you forget it.' Yet Louisa had often stayed for weekends at their house, almost a friend of the family. He was shocked that she had not written him a letter of condolence when his wife died. He sent her the newspaper notice of Daisy's death and, as a rebuke, with no comment of his own. There was no answer for a long time and then a short letter did come, signed formally Louisa Browder, saying she was sorry to read the sad news and that Daisy had been a 'loyal wife and a wonderful mother to his children'. The curt note could, of course, be called a riposte if you like to take it that way, but what struck him most was the cause of the delay in her reply. She had moved out of London. She had gone to live in this town in a house by the sea. The address transformed her: a new life in a pretty house with a sea view, that was what he repeated to himself like a song these days.

Andrews had not told Louisa he was coming: in dealing with women surprise was essential. He passed the sedate terrace houses of the sea front and was disappointed to find himself in a side street and standing at the door of a mean little villa, with no sea view and with the degrading word *Vacancies* on a card in the window. She had gone downhill. There was an old white car in the garage at the side of the place. The thumping and miauling of canned music was coming out of the front room as he pushed the door bell. There was no answer. He rang again. When the door was opened the music rushed out, swamping his voice, which he had to raise when he spoke to a gingery young man with a book in his hand. His long hair seemed to be dancing to the tune.

'Come along in,' the young man said and, bawling up the stairs 'Sally, an old gent for you,' went back to the front room. Andrews winced at the sight of linoleum on the floor of the hall. The house was cold and smelled of polish. Sarah – not Louisa – came to the top of the stairs and called out 'We're full up,' but came down, rubbing her hands together, half cringing, half ready for battle – the whole Browder family, even Louisa

(Andrews remembered) had always cringed. She said again, 'I said we're full up.' And she shut the sitting-room door before she looked at him. Then she stepped back.

'*Mr* Andrews!' she said and seemed to swallow a huge lump of unbelief and suspicion. 'What do *you* want?'

Still a public benefactor, but now hard-eyed, Andrews said, 'I was hoping to see Louisa – I happened to be here on business and I thought I'd drop in for a moment.'

'She's gone out,' said the sister, studying him. 'What do you want to see her about if I may ask? Is she expecting you?'

'No,' he said. 'Just a little surprise. When will she be in? She wrote to me so kindly when Daisy died – my wife you know.'

'I know,' said the sister briskly. 'She showed me the letter.'

'I didn't know that she had moved down here,' he said.

'I suppose she can move if she wants to,' said the sister.

'A nice little town. Really,' he said boldly, 'I've been looking around for a place for myself. You look well, Sarah.'

She did not: she looked scrawny and yellow.

'A place here?' Sarah said. 'I told you we are full.' But now she looked frightened. She studied him from his nose to the tips of his shoes. 'You mean you're looking for a *house* here?' She hesitated. At that moment the telephone on the hall table rang. 'Come into the dining-room,' she said.

She pushed him into a room and said, 'Stay there.' The room had a french window looking onto a cold little garden. The spring plants, he saw, were late this year, held back by the east wind.

He heard her answering the call: then he heard footsteps in the room above and a rush down the stairs and Louisa's voice.

'Still a liar,' said Andrews.

The room was small. The furniture was of the kind that is bought at a discount. There was a polished oak table with a dispirited runner on it, chairs that stood at the table like orphans, a sideboard with a bottle of ketchup on it. On the mantelpiece was a vase of artificial flowers and a photograph of the old Browders standing in their garden like tired and hardened pensioners. They had been a poor family, supported by Louisa, the cleverer of the daughters. There was a bleak armchair with wooden arms that dared anyone to sit on it. Andrews accepted the dare and sat, patting the arms as he waited. The call stopped and he now heard the voices of the sisters: Sarah's voice came through the door as one whispering, arguing hiss: Louisa's, saying little in her practical way, a voice warm though with iron in it. He remembered how little she had moved her lips when she spoke; even in his harassed moments with her he had admired the way the voice tersely filled his office (and even the street outside when they left the place together) with proverbial facts to be borne in mind. She had been piquant in a spinsterish way, slender, mannish

74

and brisk during the years she had worked with him in his office. It had always astonished him when his jealous wife said, 'She knows what she's after.'

Now the door was opened and in came Louisa alone, wearing a heavy grey overcoat and carrying a large handbag. It was a principle with Andrews, especially in dealing with women, to smile and put them in the wrong at once.

'Sarah told me you were out,' he said. 'I just dropped in' (this being his privilege).

'I was dressing to go out,' she said in her equally correcting way, but with a laziness that was new to him. 'Sarah says you're here on business.'

'Not really.' He smiled.

And then he came out with it, all charm: 'I came especially to see *you*, to know how things are. And to thank you for your letter.'

Except for the changeless voice, he could not believe that this dawdling woman was the Louisa he had known so well – even feared. All the way down in the train she had seemed to skip across the hedges and disappear into woods – a tall busy woman, often not more than a pair of eyebrows and big dutiful eyes. In the office she had skilfully drooped her shoulders, because he was shorter. Now, in this room, she seemed short and there was more engaging shape and body to her. Her hands, which she used to clench, were now open and at ease. Her glossy black hair was waved and though she had aged and now wore glasses, the two streaks of swan-white hair over her ears looked dashing and her lips were firm, her teeth were not set in the old attentiveness.

With no desk to work at, no papers to hand to him, no telephone to answer, no memory of detail to store for him, she stood easily free. She had often worked late at the office with him because – as he knew – she hated going back to her home. She had been good-humoured but she rarely laughed. She had lived for the office, but now the nervous lines cut by office life had gone, her face was on holiday and open.

Still, after they had talked a little, she did say with an old school-teacher's satisfied mockery: 'So you are a widower, Morton.'

She spoke of him as a species. Morton was his second name. She had never used his first Christian name, which was Alfred. That belonged to his wife at home.

'Yes,' he said, rather boasting of the fact.

'It is hard,' she said, 'to lose someone you love. I know how I felt when Mother died. I appreciated what I had lost.'

Remarkable, when one thought of her complaints about her mother. He was annoyed that he had to grimace in order to indicate that he had a tear to hold back.

He'd forgotten Daisy's jealousy of Louisa and Louisa's silence about her – except for that letter of condolence. He suddenly found himself crumpling into an account of Daisy's long illness and her death, and how a week before she died her hair seemed to be golden again, as it had been when she was a girl and how her colour came back. The tear fell and slipped into the corner of his mouth.

'And you still live in that big house?' Louisa said.

He recovered.

'No, we moved into a smaller place five years ago, when I retired.'

Louisa approved of the smaller house. 'That was wise, I'm sure.

'How do you manage by yourself?' she said without concern. 'Who looks after you?'

He had not come to talk to Louisa about this, but since his wife's death he had taken to rambling on to local people in the shops, even in the street where he lived, to anyone, about the bemusing novelty of his new life. He could not stop himself. Grief had made him novel, and he called himself 'you'.

'You get up in the morning,' he was saying to Louisa, 'if you don't forget to set the alarm the night before, and you go down and potter about in the blessed kitchen, so to speak, getting a cup of tea, and you start taking it upstairs and then you stop: you see, you can have your tea where you like, upstairs or down, and you look into the refrigerator to see what is there – sometimes things smell, go wrong. You don't cook much, you fry something perhaps, there's no decent restaurant near where we live. You forget things – don't lay the table. The laundry's the bother – a girl comes in, but these girls never clean properly and' (suddenly making a face) 'her husband has a van or something, they're up all night dancing at clubs, gambling by the sound of it, bingo or whatever they call it, some such name. Can't make a bed. Comes when she thinks she will.' And, with passion, 'No idea how to brush a carpet.'

Andrews frowned at the wall.

The gingery young man next door had turned up the volume on his record-player and the music came whirling through the wall like a typhoon that blew through his clothes into his skin. It thumped and twanged and swirled in sounds nasal and self-pitying, men groaning, girls screaming their skirts off. He held up his hand to stop the noise. Raising his voice as if to order it to stop he said, embarrassed, 'Her husband knocks her about: she showed me the bruises on her leg and on her shoulder: "Look at these bruises, they come up black and blue in the night," right up her bare leg,' he said. 'These young people laugh. I don't know what the idea is.

'I've got to get rid of that girl!' He was shouting again. For the moment he was addressing Daisy, the town, the world, and he looked startled when he saw Louisa again.

'Girls are hard to get,' Louisa said placidly. 'Sarah can't get anyone.'

'I've got to get away, sell the house,' he said. 'I was saying to Sarah a town like this would suit me,' he said. 'A blow from the sea.'

'Houses are expensive here,' she said in her book-keeping voice. 'You'd better stay where you are. You'd miss your children.'

'They've got their own lives,' he said. And he made his message clear to her. 'One thing I've learned is that you can't live in the past.'

They had been standing, but now she sat down at the table while he went back to the armchair. She had loosened her overcoat, as if to let out the woman in her, but she held on to the handbag standing on the table.

The music had stopped strangling the air but it had fallen into long hiccuping passages of monotonous indifferent drumming. The sound was like the sound of the wheels of the train when he had come up in the morning and when the trees had looked girlish in the fields and he had imagined her as she used to be, before the quarrel – a friend, more intelligent than poor Daisy had been. He had looked out of the window of the train, once just in time to catch sight of a wide estuary where the sailing boats were moored, and in that glimpse of the sea he saw it had lost its air of heaving and grieving at its stored-up deaths. It was waving like a flag. It had struck him when he walked up from the station that the shopping street of the town was full of men and women whose arms and legs had been coiled up in bed with one another all night. Scores of women passed him, women you didn't know but who might slap your face if you stopped them and explained your situation. Yet, as they hurried by, they seemed to ask you why you didn't. What could you say? How do you begin it? You have to get to know them – the boredom of that – at his age he hadn't time for that sort of thing. The one woman he knew was this Louisa – she knew him and he knew her. In a funny sort of way they had had years of marriage in the office.

In the room he was arguing with the drumming, which went on and on, and he was even tapping his foot. Louisa looked years away from him at the table. The crowds of women in the streets and shops had been too near, too sudden, but the distance of Louisa made him stop tapping his foot. He crossed his legs and felt the imposing stillness of a desire that he had never felt before. Desire in a cheap place like this!

He said, in an unnaturally high voice, going back to what he had already said, 'Sarah looks well, and so do you.'

'Thank you,' said Louisa. 'She is.'

'You must have a lot to do, running this place,' he said. 'She said you were full-up.'

'I believe she is,' said Louisa. 'Everything in the town gets full-up in the holidays. I don't *live* here, you know,' she said with a small condescending laugh.

'I thought you did,' he said, feeling in his pocket for her letter.

'No, I'm at the hotel,' she said. 'More comfortable. We sold the old house in London when mother died.'

Moved to a hotel! She seemed to leave her distance and come closer to him. As a salesman he had spent so much of his life in hotels. He loved, of course, those great acres of carpets in the grand ones; hotels were palaces of pleasure and money. Their very upholstery sent messages of erotic sensation when one touched it. Even in the small hotel – in a town like this – the guests, the waiters, the servants and the clerks, were like figures in a dream as they walked silently from room to room. When telephones rang they carried voices from another world. One became a dream oneself.

'I was going to say,' he said, showing his new admiration of her worth, 'that this place did not seem like you.'

And he waved disparagingly at the furniture.

'You've done what I ought to do.' He shouted for a

third time decisively at the music. 'Are you at the George?' he challenged. 'Don't tell me you're at the George!' He laughed. 'I had lunch there today. Very comfortable. Good fish. I didn't see *you*!'

He uncrossed his legs and felt himself become a wonder.

'No,' she said, smiling at him mischievously: her first real smile. 'I'm up the hill near the church. The Clarence. Quieter. More select.'

'Sea view?' he said greedily.

'Of course – every room – and a nice garden.'

It was yet another principle of his never to be at a loss. He pulled a list of local hotels from his pocket.

'Yes, here it is. The Clarence, thirty-seven rooms, all with sea view.'

Louisa said, 'Forty-five pounds a day. With bath. Service and VAT not included. Weekly terms.'

'That's right,' said Andrews. And, congratulating her: 'Pricey.'

'Not for what you get,' she said.

The Browders had been a poor skimping family, carefully putting money away. Extraordinary. Louisa must have saved a lot to be staying in an hotel like the Clarence.

'Why don't we have dinner there tonight? Let me buy you dinner,' he said grandly.

'I can't do that, Morton,' she said.

'Or at the George,' he said, 'if you want a change. Funny thing about the George – they have got that carpet, like the one I sold when we were at Brighton years ago, one of our lines, the Demeter Floral –

chocolate and flowers. You remember it I'm sure. Chrysanthemums in an urn.'

He laughed eagerly.

'It will be just like old times.'

Louisa frowned at that.

'Morton, I'm not *staying* at the Clarence. I'm not a guest. I work there in the office. We're very busy. I've got to go in a minute and see about the dinners. Twelve Germans have just booked in. That was reception ringing up when you were talking to Sarah.'

Louisa diminished in his eyes. He gaped.

'Working there? Did you say working?' said Andrews. He was offended with her because he had made a mistake. He turned on the boy next door. 'I wish Sarah would make that boy stop his infernal noise. You can't hear what anyone says.'

Louisa frowned at him.

'Oh that! That's Peter, my step-son, he's working for his exams. He always puts his record-player on when he's working. I'm used to it, I suppose, but it gets on his father's nerves. That's why we send Peter down here to Sarah's, but he eats with us at the hotel. When you run a hotel you have to put the guests first.'

'Step-son?' he said.

The air seemed to go out of his lungs with a whistle and his voice went up high as a boy's, and she seemed to him to jump up and down, like a film gone wrong, between floor and ceiling.

'I am a step-mother,' she pronounced, as one who was equipped with a two-fisted power.

Andrews felt himself clamped between the arms of

the narrow chair. His mouth was left open with no words in it, a foolish red hole he could not close. It seemed to him that she was not one woman but had become part of the general chorus of women he had seen in the streets of the town, impersonally swinging their handbags and lugging their shopping bags, taunting him with their indifference. In his bewilderment he lost all sense of time as he often did through living alone, and was on the point of saying aloud 'Daisy will have a fit when I tell her this.'

He recovered enough to say, 'I don't believe you.'

A rival widower had stolen a march on him! There was also the affront that, as a former employee and office possession, she had not consulted him first.

He felt in his pocket for her letter, which lately he had taken to carrying about, as a kind of invoice. He took it out and, putting on his glasses, read it. Looking over the top of his glasses he said, 'You didn't say you were married here.'

It was signed with her maiden name.

'I wasn't married then,' she said, formally. 'Mr Forrester and I were married last year – when his divorce came through.'

Louisa fattened with pride when she threw out the word 'divorce'. She was conveying that she was not a consoling nurse or frustrated spinster, fit only for an enfeebled widower. She was not a victim! She had attracted a man so much that he had divorced his wife. There was a note of rebuke in this: what had Andrews done for her? Casually she dropped the subject.

'My husband *manages* the Clarence. We belong to a

chain.' The word 'chain' enlarged her importance. 'So does the George. When we are full up we can always send people down there.'

Andrews could manage only a faint sarcasm.

'You seem to own the town,' he said.

Not leaving the matter there she pretended to be hurt. 'I don't know why you are so surprised, Morton. Actually you have *met* my husband.'

He was in the dock, accused. As coolly as he could he said: '*Met* him? I don't think I have – where – what is his name?'

'The same as mine,' she said. 'Forrester. Jack Forrester.'

He felt in his pocket again, but gave up.

'I don't remember any Forrester,' he said.

'Oh, Morton!' she said archly. 'Think! Brighton! June '74. The trade exhibition. When you got that big contract for Demeter Floral. You remember *that*, I'm sure.'

There they were, bang in the middle of their quarrel. Surely, after all these years, she was not going to drag that up?

'I remember I pulled off a £10,000 order,' he boasted.

He could at any rate dismiss her marriage.

'I am not talking about carpets,' she said between her teeth. Her eyes, which were made larger by her glasses, seemed to him to be rummaging into their working life together, as if it were a waste. A question was in her eyes, idly put there to gratify some private vanity.

He was not going to be fool enough, in his present situation, to gratify that.

He knew the stare was unforgiving, that she might

force her question upon him. He had smoothed away all his memories of that incomprehensible time at Brighton but now he remembered going back to the hotel where they had been staying, and that she had been waiting in the foyer for him. He remembered her saying with excitement, 'Did you bring it off?' And he had said, 'Let's get out of this.' They had crossed the street to the promenade, and he remembered the long, gaudy, floodlit sea front with the flags flying from the hotels and from the tall lamp standards and how the lights had blacked out all sight of the sea. The front was like a stage set: the crowd looked clownish as they passed from lamp to lamp. She had put her arm on his as he talked about his success. Usually at trade exhibitions they dined at the hotel with people in the trade and early in the evening she left him with the men, but this night she had persuaded him to celebrate at a restaurant. They drank a glass or two of champagne and then they dawdled back to the hotel, and she had circumspectly taken her pinching hand from his arm as they went across the foyer to the lift; but there she held his arm again and squeezed it as they went up to their floor. At the door of her room, rather embarrassingly, she had kept him talking, her voice getting quieter. Her fingers pretended to pick a piece of cotton from the lapel of his jacket.

'Come in for a minute,' she mumbled, as if she were eating. And there was an eating look in her eyes.

Andrews had been startled. He remembered thinking he ought not to have let her drink champagne. He had looked at his watch and said: 'Good God! Do you know

what time it is? I haven't rung Daisy yet to tell her the
news. I'm late.'

It was then he saw her face turn and there had
been a twist of anger on it. It became suddenly hard,
empty-eyed, like a mask of brass in the sick yellow light
of the hotel corridor as he said good night in a fatherly
way and went down to his own room at the end of
the corridor. He was surprised that she banged her
door. He was glad: he couldn't sit up half the night
with her talking about the troubles of the Browder
family.

But the next day! Andrews had never been able to
tell his wife what happened on the second evening.
Daisy wouldn't have believed him. She would have
shouted triumphantly that she had 'known it' for years.
That evening contained a lump of his history, so heavy
in his mind, so entangled in outrage and the inadmissible
desire he had never recognised, that he had succeeded
in locking it out of memory. Now, talking to this married
Louisa, in this miserable little villa by the sea, every
fragment of it came alive again.

The day after their 'celebration', Louisa was late at
the firm's stand at the show. Not surprisingly, she had
a headache. He told her to go and lie down. He himself
was so taken up with the details of his sale that he didn't
get back to his own room at the hotel until seven in the
evening. When he got there the telephone was ringing.
That pest Sarah! The Browder family up in arms! Where
was Louisa? Sarah said she had been ringing all day.
Their mother was ill again. Dying, of course. Old Mrs
Browder was said to be dying in every call Sarah had

made for years. Louisa must come home at once. If she did go, there was never anything wrong with Mrs Browder.

To cut Sarah short, he had said, 'I'm sure she's in her room. There must be some mistake. I'll go and see.'

And he did go and knocked and knocked at the door, for he could hear voices. He heard a man's voice call, 'Who the hell is that? Tell him to go away.'

Louisa came to the door in a yellow dressing-gown – very yellow.

'It's only Mr Andrews,' she called back to a red-haired man who came out of the bathroom, saying, 'Tell him to buzz off and mind his own business.'

The man had a necktie in his hand and was bare-footed. The scene had been so incredible to Andrews that he had scarcely recognised Louisa. He could not now remember if he said anything to her, but he congratulated himself on remembering the exact words he had said to the man: 'I am addressing my secretary. Her mother is very ill.'

'I'll ring Sarah later, Mr Andrews' was all Louisa said. 'She's always checking up on me.'

And she had shut the door in his face.

Even then he did not believe what he had seen. He went to his room. He rang Sarah and in a muddled way said first that Louisa was asleep and then that she was with friends.

'That's a lie,' said Sarah. 'She's with you. I can hear her. Do you think I don't know what's going on between you?'

Andrews had had enough of the Browders. He lost his temper.

'If you want to know, she's picked up some man in the bar,' he said.

Sarah astounded him by laughing.

'That will stop you messing about, won't it? I've always been sorry for your wife.'

Now, in Sarah's house, with the old Browders looking at him from their photograph on the mantelpiece, he saw Louisa was waiting for him to speak.

'You told Sarah you *had* met him,' she said. 'It was not very nice of you, Morton. He is my husband now, so really, you see, it might be awkward to have dinner with you. Really I don't think this town would suit you, do you? And now I must go and you must catch your train. Sarah's taking me to the Clarence and she'll drop you at the station. Was there anything else you wanted to ask me?'

'Nothing,' he said.

The handle of the door moved. Sarah, he guessed, had been listening at the door, for in she came and said, 'Now then, Louisa, your husband's rung again.'

In the car Louisa said to Sarah, 'Tell Peter to remember to put on a tie if he's coming up to dinner.'

Nothing more was said.

Andrews watched her go into the Clarence, of course – but nothing, nothing, nothing, the wheels of the train hammered, like Sarah's voice, as he was carried back to London. Passing the estuary in the dusk he saw the boats were flying no pennants and no flags.

THINGS

I was out early practising my putting on the lawn, which I have brought pretty well to perfection. This was the first time I had had a chance to get out my clubs after a week of gales. They strike this jagged tip of south-west England first, tear through the leaning trees and send the fields and hedges streaming and the steep hills bowling across the map into the Channel, and take your mind and the tears in your eyes away with them. But now, as if the whole rumpus had not occurred, the sky was cloudless and as still as glass, and the only sounds were the tap of my club on the balls and the cries of the gulls ripping through the air. The young gulls must have hatched and the parents were driving off the crows. Probably next day there would be sea fog. We don't live on land here, as my wife says, we live in weather. One lives from one hour to the next, as they turn into days and weeks and the piled up years we spent in Africa, Canada, Egypt and Hong Kong.

On this quiet day last April Rhoda rang up. It was
the first time that we had been able to have breakfast
outside. As I say, I was out on the lawn and I heard the
telephone ring. I am supposed to be retired, but the
week rarely passes without two or three calls from the
London office, the dockyard or some Ministry about an
oil rig or a dry dock or asking me to go and serve on
some commission of enquiry. I am a consultant now,
called in when something goes wrong – stress mostly.

I crossed the lawn. My wife, Miranda, was standing
by an open window answering the call. Not in her usual
calm, practical voice, but in a high thrilled rushing voice:
'Darling, how extraordinary! How marvellous! Where
are you? What are you doing? Why didn't you write?
We've been so worried about you. What *are* you
doing . . .?' and so on, as she used to do when she and
I first met and she was in love. She looked younger and
warmer with every word.

Rhoda is her sister, who lives in Italy. Miranda was,
I supposed, shouting to be heard in the Mediterranean.
She always shouts on an international call. But she was
really proclaiming, in her emotional way, across time,
and that is why she was looking so young. We haven't
seen Rhoda since we went to Hong Kong about ten
years ago and, frankly, it's been a relief. She has never
been one to write – a Christmas card every year, of
course, but nothing more. When the long call came to
an end Miranda stood staring out over the fields into
the sky and to the sea. Then she came back out of time
when she saw me.

I said: 'Has anything happened? Something wrong?

It must have cost her a penny or two ringing from Italy.'

We often laughed at Rhoda's comic miserliness over small sums of money.

'She's not in Italy,' said Miranda, accusing Rhoda, me, and the view with one of her dramatic stares. 'She's on her way down from London. She's in Exeter. I've asked her to stay the night. She's sad the children are not here: she was longing to see them.'

There was a pause as her excitement died.

'She *is* incredible,' Miranda said. 'She said she didn't know they were both married. But I wrote her – you saw the letter – she even sent them wedding presents!'

'Typical Rhoda,' I said. 'She lives in the future.'

Miranda frowned at me. 'Be nice,' she pleaded.

I was going to say, 'I hope she's not bringing that awful man Sammy she's living with, the one with the wide trousers,' but I checked myself. I retreated into a joke that goes back to the time when I first met Miranda and when Rhoda was no more than a child.

'I wonder,' I said, 'what she *wants*,' pronouncing that word in Rhoda's baby-talk way when she was very determined, dwelling on it – 'wawnt'. Her telephone call had opened up the past for Miranda and me. Miranda laughed.

'I bet she'll *wawnt* our house,' I added.

Miranda said firmly, 'Well, she can't have that.'

We are very proud of our house. We are in our sixties, though Miranda does not look it: her hair is brown and has scarcely any grey, but the house has rejuvenated us. After working for so long abroad, living as we had to in hotels, company bungalows and other people's furnished flats and villas, with nothing of our own there, now for about the first time we have a place that is really our own and with our own things. New sofas, beds, chairs – we are still as excited as if we were newly married. We came here because Miranda was born and brought up in this part of the country, in a house called Lodge seventeen miles away, a place which had been in her family for something like a hundred years – or even more, I suppose. We have the portrait of her great-great-grandfather the 'Trafalgar Captain', who retired from the Navy there after that war. The picture hangs in our living-room now. Lodge is where I first met the family during *our* war. In the invasion scare I was billeted in the stables. We were wiring the beaches and building those concrete strong points – pill-boxes – along the coast.

Miranda and I sometimes pass Lodge on our way to London. You can't see it from the road because the trees and shrubberies are overgrown. You can't even see the stump of brick tower that her grandfather built at one end of the place, in a fit of pretension, for the house is no more than a square farmhouse built of narrow slabs of brown and black stone. The trees darkened the rooms even in Miranda's time, and the troops used to get scared by the squeaking branches scraping the slates at night. Miranda loved Lodge and was sad that the place, so settled and with windows that still, for her, seemed to hold the faces that had looked through them, was sold when her mother died. Rhoda detested it – or so she said.

Our own house is, I am glad to say, modern and

pretty with its pink walls, and I have improved it. I am efficient at this kind of thing, and Miranda has furnished it with taste. Living here, we often say, is like having a second honeymoon. We live for ourselves and know hardly any of the summer people who come down, though I meet one or two on the golf course. Of course we have our own children and grand-children down in the summer. Thick walls of flowering shrubs ten feet high – which I keep well clipped – protect Miranda's garden where she is always working when she is not painting a little. Painting got her through the loneliness of being abroad. Here, since this is her own country and she isn't lonely, she paints less. She says the light changes too fast for her now.

So Rhoda came to stay.

We both say still that we did not recognise Rhoda, except for her walk on the gravel drive, perhaps. She trotted like a busy little girl as she got out of her car, went sniffing around it, peering in, seeing the doors were locked. (She kept everything locked when she was a child.) Then she stepped onto the lawn in the high-heeled shoes she always wears to give her height and stood back like an impertinent urchin staring at our house, counting the windows – she had always been a counting girl. Then, chin still lifted, her nose wriggled and she sniffed – a good sign with her: she admired the place! I was right: she was the old Rhoda, still 'wawnt-ing' until plaintiveness quickly followed.

But she was not any of the series of Rhodas we have in our memory of her, certainly not the Rhoda I had last seen in my bank in London, ten years before, when

she was off to Italy. Like Miranda's, her hair was brown
when she was a girl, but in the bank it was yellow and
on it she was wearing a small black flowerpot hat. She
had always been one for a fashion that had gone out
and with her smudged lipstick, her hit-or-miss eye-
shadow, she looked at that time like a widow who had
not yet mastered the part. Naturally: she was unmarried.
There was a red-faced man with a hot-from-a-funeral
look with her. (I will come back to Sammy later on.)
But this was not the Rhoda we now saw on our lawn.
We had expected sunburn, an Italian look, but instead
her little face was scalded and she wore no makeup.
The flowerpot hat had been replaced by a man's shabby
brown beret, tipped forward on her head, and from
under it poured a long stream of hair, grey as fog, over
her shoulders and down her back. She was wearing
something like a brown-striped football jersey and
bright emerald-green trousers, and she now had a small
belly full of impudence and authority. She looked like
a witch out of a child's book. I did not say this to
Miranda as we walked towards her, but I did say,
'Rhoda still wants justice.' (She had always said in her
quarrels: 'It isn't fair. I want justice.')

Rhoda trotted up to us, the kissing began, and then
abruptly she stepped back and considered me.

'You've grown a beard,' she mocked. (I have a
pointed white beard.) 'You look pink and respectable.'

'Oh,' laughed Miranda, 'he's not as respectable as he
looks.'

'You see?' cried Rhoda with glee, turning to me. 'She
got her dig in.'

94

Rhoda has always been conspicuous for a few key words. After 'want' came 'dig': she loved to see people getting 'digs' in at each other.The next word came out when I asked, 'Where's your suitcase?' and looked into the back of her car. A pile of old cardboard boxes and tied-up packages had been tumbled in. On top of them were a radio, two umbrellas, a couple of pairs of slacks, an anorak, two tins of biscuits, Wellington boots and a stack of steel rods wrapped in canvas which looked like golf clubs. And a rolled-up sleeping-bag.

'I didn't know you played golf,' I said.

'No, that's my bed. I can't sleep in hotel beds. I put it on the floor. I stopped in Exeter on the way down.'

'Been making tea?' I asked. There was a teapot on the floor.

'I picked it up in Taunton market,' she said. She had a plastic bag in her hand.

'Nothing in the car?' I said.

'No, those are my *things*,' she said holding the bag tightly.

'Things' was another word that went back to her childhood. I remember the chest of drawers in her room at Lodge and – more important – one or two boxes containing her broken watches and dolls, strips of velvet or silk, patterns, knitting, sewing, badges, clips, combs, childish jewellery, letters, programmes, the crown of a hat she had once had, a mug, unused diaries and cracked snapshots, dozens of cotton reels. No one in the family – certainly not Miranda or a maid (there were maids when she was a child) – was allowed near the hoard.

Once I remember her mother saying, 'You must clear this mess up. What's the good of *one* king?' – holding up a playing-card – and Rhoda snatched it from her mother, put it into a cardboard box and sat on it. 'It's mine.'

We were about to move into the house when she stopped and pointed back to our white gate. 'Philip,' she said, 'I say! Pebbles! Was that your idea?'

'It's the name of the house. What about it? Down the road there's Breakers, White Sands, Sea Spray, The Dunes.'

'Weird!' Rhoda mocked.

'I don't see anything weird in it,' I said. 'You have Bella Vista all over Italy.'

'Sammy and I live in a flat,' she said and then turned to Miranda and said, 'Sammy is my lover.'

'I know,' said Miranda. 'Philip told me.'

'Lover' is the last and most important of Rhoda's key words. She did not live in time, as we did; the coming and going of lovers marked the calendar for her. We did not know many of Rhoda's friends, but I cannot think of any man of whom she did not casually make this claim or, at any rate, did not consider whether she might wish to make it at some time or other. Sammy had lasted longer than most.

'I wish you'd brought Sammy,' said Miranda. 'I've never met him, you know. You didn't leave him in Exeter, did you?'

'No, he's in Rome. I expect he's still in bed. He was fast asleep when I left.'

'I'll get some tea,' I said.

'No, I want to see the house first. Everything,' said Rhoda and she put on her strong glasses for the inspection.

I let Miranda take her. I could hear them going from room to room upstairs, talking and laughing. I went up at last to see how they were getting on. They came out of a bedroom and I pointed to the radiators and said: 'Have you shown Rhoda the bathrooms?' They ignored me. I went along to the first bathroom and, since they didn't follow, I flushed the lavatory.

Rhoda said, 'Why did you do that?'

'He loves doing it,' said Miranda. 'He'll never stop being an engineer.'

'Not like those awful lavatories at Lodge,' I called, 'where the pipes clanked all over the house and you thought it was coming down, or like that one in Cairo: that was the worst.'

'It's like a second honeymoon being here,' said Miranda – *our* phrase.

'I never had one. Everything else, but not that. I mean you can't count Jeremy,' said Rhoda, walking slowly along the landing and peering at each engraving on the wall.

'"Poachers Netting Partridges at Night",' she read aloud. 'That was at Lodge. In the hall.'

We got down to the sitting-room – it was once two rooms and is now large, and from the two west windows there is a clear sight of the sea and the Pig Rock, lying two miles out with its moustache of surf. Some days when bad weather is coming the rock seems to move in, dark and near: on this afternoon it glittered and seemed farther away. It's the first thing I look at when I get up in the morning, better than a barometer.

I mentioned this, but Rhoda, who had not taken off her beret, did not reply. She was standing still in the sitting-room, which I consider Miranda's masterpiece: she ought to have been a decorator, she has such a gift for colour. Rhoda was counting again. In that jersey and those terrible emerald trousers, she stood out like a gypsy. Quick as a bird she picked out the one or two family things that had come to us from Lodge. She stared at the portrait of the Trafalgar Captain over the fireplace and said suddenly, 'I looked in on old George Ogbourne in Exeter.'

'I wondered why you stopped in Exeter,' Miranda said. 'You should have come straight through. Who is George Ogbourne?'

'Oh, you know him,' said Rhoda. 'He used to be at Raddles, the auctioneers who sold Lodge when the Bulwers bought it. Those auction people make the money! He went in for antiques. He remembers *you*, Miranda. And he remembered me. "Let me see, you must be Rhoda," he said.

'He's getting on,' she said. 'His son Peter runs the business now. He knows the Bulwers. You didn't tell me that Jeremy Bulwer had married again when his wife died – that fluffy little thing. What is the new one like?'

'We don't know the Bulwers,' I said. 'I just see him on the golf course sometimes. Very bald.'

'But Jeremy was my first lover!' she said, forgetting us and the room for a moment, and she took a step or two, looking at her feet as if talking to one foot and then the other, plotting. And then she said sentimentally, 'I think I'll drop in at the Lodge while I'm here. For old times' sake.'

This silenced us. I know that thirty years have passed and that, thank God, Rhoda's love affairs are no business of ours. But this was too near home. I could just imagine Rhoda 'dropping in' at Lodge and getting in a sizeable 'dig', saying what a funny thing it was – that Jeremy had been mad about her and they'd run off to London when he was engaged to his first wife, who in the end had taken him back. And then adding loudly what she used to say of all her early lovers – 'He was impotent' – to see how the Bulwers took that.

'We shall have to stop that,' I thought. Very embarrassing on a golf course. Almost as bad as the time I was persuaded to take Rhoda on in our London office and she fell for Doggett and his wife asked Miranda to intervene. If she *has* come back to start those old larks, I thought, I'll have something to say about it and she won't like it.

But Rhoda was chattering on.

'Peter Ogbourne says prices have gone sky high since we sold Lodge.' And looking at a china cabinet in the room she said, 'You'd get a thousand or more for a piece like that. I gave Peter a lift to Plymouth, his car had broken down. He was going to a sale.'

'I don't think we're selling anything, are we, Miranda?' I said coldly.

Miranda said, 'Why don't we all sit down?'

Rhoda studied the positions of the sofa and armchairs

and then she looked closely at one of the chairs, which had a footstool under it.

'My darling little stool!' she cried. She darted to it, knelt down and pulled it out, and sat on it victoriously. I have never seen an object 'bagged' so quickly in my life.

'Yes,' said Miranda. 'Granny's little stool.' And to me: 'Rhoda and I used to fight for it. Granny made us take turns.'

'Granny always cheated,' said Rhoda, dropping her mouth open and looking from one to the other of us to see if the 'dig' had got home.

What I remembered, as I went out to get the tea tray, was Rhoda at the age of fifteen in school uniform sitting on the stool at Lodge before Miranda and I were married, staring at love, as we sat on a terrible prickly horsehair sofa, and Rhoda saying, 'Why don't you hold hands?' At fifteen she was a pest who followed us everywhere. She had just become very religious: one of the maids had converted her to the Plymouth Brethren. 'But, darling,' her mother said, 'they're not quite our class.' Rhoda's religious phase lasted until the second year of the war when the invasion scare came and the soldiers were billeted in the stables. One of them, a Captain Blake, called her the pocket Cleopatra. (It was in her Plymouth Brethren period that she had once left the room calling out 'Sexual intercourse is damnation'. She loved the phrase: it was directed at us.)

I put the tray down. Rhoda gazed at the silver teapot and then shook a passing fancy out of her head.

'If I had married Jeremy Bulwer I'd have had Lodge,'

she said. And picking up a scone, she waved it at the room and said, 'Did you take all this to Africa?'

'No. Of course not. Most of it's new. We left one or two Lodge things with Philip's mother,' said Miranda. 'There wasn't much – the cabinet, the Trafalgar Captain, the secretaire . . .'

'I suppose you took everything to Italy,' Miranda said. 'It would be easier.'

'Oh no,' said Rhoda, buttering her scone. 'We sold it all.'

'Everything, after you left the Square when . . .' Miranda began nervously.

'Yes, Sammy and I sold the lot when we bought the hotel.'

'All of it? Oh, Rhoda!'

'We ought to have kept the silver,' Rhoda said. 'We'd have got ten times the price now. Money is money, isn't it? As Sammy says, no good hoarding everything. Things need a change. It cheers them up, he says.'

'It's cheered up the Captain coming here, I must say,' I said pointing to the portrait. 'You couldn't see him properly at Lodge. We had him cleaned.'

Rhoda sniffed at the Captain. 'Imagine the life of his wife, polishing all that stuff, chained to it, while he was at sea,' Rhoda said.

'But you used to love *things*, Rhoda,' said Miranda. 'It seems so sad but I suppose it was sensible. There wouldn't have been enough room in your hotel.'

'We've sold the hotel,' said Rhoda. 'All those tourists taking photographs and talking about "art". It was too much for Sammy's nerves – I mean the old people you get always complaining about their washbasins and quarrelling with one another, some are quite mad. And the bells going all day.'

Miranda said, in her discreet, orderly way, 'We've never been quite sure what Sammy *does*. I do so wish you'd brought him with you. What does he *do* now?'

Miranda had never quite believed my account of Sammy when I came back from our accidental meeting so long ago at my bank. What had struck me particularly in the fleshy young man was his trousers: his jacket was open and the trousers were braced high over his wide waist, almost to his ribs. He had black hair with a curl over his forehead and a damp, glistening crimson face, his fists, his nose, his lips were heavy; his body looked too full of blood, like that of a boxer or a publican or one of the security guards at the bank. Rhoda had said: 'I want you to meet Sammy. He's my lover.' They looked as though they had hired each other. He came forward and said 'Pleased to meet you,' in a confidential way that suggested: this bird and I have just done a deal. And he looked back shrewdly at the bank clerks at the main desk as he might have glanced back at a bar when he was going to offer a new pal a drink.

'We are in a rush,' Rhoda had said. 'We've only got half an hour to get to the airport. We're going to Italy.'

'S'right,' Sammy said.

Rhoda looked proudly amused by the disparity of their accents – a 'dig' at me, of course.

'Come on,' she said to Sammy, and he lazily followed her steps out of the bank.

Sammy called back to me, 'Be seeing you.'

One thing I was certain of: he was afraid of Rhoda.

Now, as Rhoda was passing her cup to Miranda, she said: 'He's got a nightclub now. It's much better for him. Poor Sammy, he's allergic to the sun in Italy. It upsets his eyes. He's shortsighted. He likes night work – he sleeps all day.'

I remembered how the hulking fellow blinked when he was introduced to me. I had said to Miranda when I got home, 'Rhoda's shortsighted too. They probably don't see each other.'

'We get a crowd,' Rhoda was saying now, 'especially at the weekends.'

Her businesslike words brought to Rhoda's little eyes that miserly gleam the family used to tease her about at Lodge, which had evidently lasted: the clothes she was wearing looked cheap. But the plaintive drooping mouth of her 'wawnting' was not there. Her lips curled up happily when she talked of Sammy.

'Money is very necessary to Sammy, you know,' she said to me.

'We all need money nowadays,' I answered, laughing.

'You don't understand, Philip,' she said. 'He needs it for his gambling.'

'Oh, Rhoda, you don't mean you've got a gambling club?' cried Miranda.

'He doesn't drink. He doesn't even drink wine in Italy. He doesn't mind if I do. He needs to gamble,' Rhoda added, 'psychologically.'

'Oh, Rhoda, I don't know. Isn't it awful for you? I know those places make money, but they lose more. It's lucky you haven't a family.'

'But I have,' Rhoda said. 'There's Sammy's little boy. He's sweet. He calls me Mamita.'

'We didn't know Sammy was married before,' we said together.

'He wasn't. He had an Italian woman,' said Rhoda.

And she sat back looking from one to the other of us with a storyteller's glee. She sighed.

'How nice it is here. D'you remember how we used to go up the cliffs to watch the baby seagulls? Will you take me, Philip, while I'm here?'

'I am sure Philip will take you,' said Miranda. 'When he's done his letters.'

I took the hint and went to my study. There was a photograph of an oil rig being towed out to sea on one wall and a watercolour of boats on Hong Kong harbour, one of Miranda's, but all I could think of was Rhoda's long grey hair over her shoulders. 'She's mad. She's mad. It's the usual tale of an old woman trying to look young, being bled for her money by a layabout.' The scene in my bank kept racing across the page as I started to write a letter, and I had to give up. Perhaps Sammy had sent her over here to get money out of Miranda?

An hour went by and then Miranda opened my door and, looking back cautiously, said loudly, 'Are you ready now to take Rhoda to see the baby seagulls while I start cooking?'

Miranda looked behind her, listened, and then whispered, 'I think she's looking for a house.'

'Here? Oh, God! Not here!'

'She's on about starting an antique shop . . .' – but

she stopped as we heard Rhoda's heels in the hall.

'He'd love to take you, Rhoda,' Miranda called.

Rhoda and I got into the car. When the sun goes down into the sea here it often sets off a firework display, sending out pink rockets, but this evening there was no more than a slow, yellowing light above a bank of low cloud that was coming in. The daylight was going and the sea was as dull as slate.

'It's going to be too late to see the baby seagulls,' I said as we slowed down at the turning to the cliff.

'I don't care whether I see them or not,' Rhoda said. 'Peter and I will see them tomorrow – Peter Ogbourne. I've got to get off early. I'm picking up Peter and we're driving to Falmouth. He's got another sale there. Let's go to Lodge.'

So all this talk of seagulls was a trick to get me to Lodge, to 'drop in' on the Bulwers. I was not going to have that. 'Just to pass it,' she said wistfully. I was wrong.

So the drive was to be a sentimental trip on a cloudy evening. There is something bemusing about the narrow roads in this part of the country. A stranger can easily get lost in them, they wind between banks of stone slabs with high hedges on top of them, so that you are tunnelling and see nothing of the country, simply the sky. North, south, east and west vanish. At the sharp corners there are often signposts showing four ways, with different distances, for getting to the same village. Tourists laugh at them, forgetting these roads were built not for getting from village to village but from farm to farm. The only dramatic sight is the number of dead

trees one passes, tall silver skeletons with their branch-
ing arms stuck up, like dead preachers.

Rhoda was counting the skeleton trees with excitement. She said, 'There is one at Lodge.'

And so there was.

'I'll slow down. I can't stop – it's a nasty corner,' I
said, for I was still suspicious. 'You won't be able to see
anything.'

'That's all right,' she said again. 'Just to feel myself
passing it.'

The sight contented her, and very slowly we passed
the gate of the overgrown drive.

The old concrete pill-box we had built just inside the
drive during the war was still there, but with nettles
growing out of it now. The sight of that pleased Rhoda
too. She used to stand there watching us build it.

'I liked the war,' she said. 'It was fun. Very good for
women.'

'Not for your mother or anyone with children,' I said.
'No more servants. They went into the factories.'

'That's what I mean,' she said. 'They got decent wages
for once. Mother was hell to the village girls we had.'

'Women have a worse time now,' I said.

We got into the usual argument but she rattled on
until she suddenly stopped and said, 'Do you remember
Captain Blake? He turned me out of the tower. I was
furious with him – putting a machine-gun post up there.
Stupid idea. It was *my* room. I had all my things there.
I think that's where I lost my Coronation mug.'

Her indignation died.

'Poor Captain Blake. Why did they *arrest* him?'

I could have said, 'You know why, Rhoda. Don't look so innocent,' but she carried on.

'I know he was rather – you know – but he really did *like* little girls. He was only cuddly. He called me the pocket Venus.'

I said I thought it was the pocket Cleopatra.

'No,' she said fiercely. 'It was Venus.'

We had now passed the gate, thank God, and had gone beyond the wood at the end of what used to be the garden.

She closed the window of the car and tidied her hair, spreading it carefully over her shoulders, looking like a witch once again, and said, 'By the way, Peter is not my lover. Actually I'm not interested in sex anymore.'

This was the most startling remark I had ever heard Rhoda make.

'I didn't think he was,' I said laughing. 'You've only known him a day.'

'Two days,' she said.

We were back in the maze of high-banked lanes, and I put the headlights on.

'I showed the children to Peter,' she suddenly said. 'I've got them in the car.'

A home-going tractor with no lights came suddenly out of a blind side turning when she said this and I had to brake suddenly.

'Bloody fool,' I called out. 'What do you mean – children?'

'The Captain's children – the picture with his wife. They're in the back of my car. I brought them with me. Peter says I ought to take them to Sotheby's and get them valued, they'd fetch a good price. Did Miranda tell you? Sammy and I are going in for antiques – not in Italy, Italy's finished.'

And then she said, 'I *saw* that in Exeter.' She was talking to herself, not to me.

'Saw' was a word of hers I had forgotten. It is really the most important. When Rhoda 'sees', she is having a sudden vision or revelation, which comes into her mind out of the blue, driving out all calculation for the moment. I think it must have started in her religious phase and was something she got from the Brethren, something like a 'call', although you hear a 'call' but you 'see' a vision. Miranda and I used to be distressed or angry about the mess she seemed to make of her life – those 'lovers' always left her, she did not leave them, and then her money was obviously being thrown away on Sammy; it seemed to us a bad end to it. What kept her going were these sudden 'seeings'.

'I don't know anything about shops. I'm an engineer. Don't shops require capital? I don't know anything about antiques.'

'But Peter does,' she said.

I knew what was going to happen as our headlights lit up our pink house. Rhoda would rush in to Miranda, alight with vision, and say that I had said the idea was splendid.

That is almost what happened when I was getting the drinks and Miranda came in from the kitchen. Miranda and I exchanged glances: What has she told you? What do you know? Did Miranda think Rhoda and Sammy were breaking up? What about this Peter? What was

going on? Miranda was signalling: I don't know. Do
you? We were like actors sketching our way through
lines in a plot that only Rhoda knew. I said, to forestall
Rhoda, 'No baby seagulls.'

'We went to Lodge,' said Rhoda.

'Just passed it,' I said, to calm Miranda.

Rhoda paid no attention to us.

'I'll get the children,' she said and carrying her drink
with her, she went out to her car.

I said to Miranda quickly: 'The Captain's children.
She's going to sell the picture.'

Rhoda returned, holding her glass high in one hand
and carrying the picture, which was nearly as tall as
herself. It was wrapped in old sacking and roughly tied.
She put it against a chair and swallowed her drink, then
she knelt down and started picking at the string. Bits of
the dirty sacking made a mess on the carpet. I tried to
pick it up. I hate a mess in a room. We saw the picture
at last.

Unlike our portrait of the Trafalgar Captain, this
picture was quite large – we always said that was why
Rhoda had chosen it. It was exactly as it had been at
Lodge – darkened by age, which made the faces small
and yellow. The Captain's wife was sitting on a stone
bench, under a tree, and with her were three little
girls in once-white dresses with blue ribbons, one child
looking down at a little dog. A country scene but, rather
absurdly, the painter had put in the mast of a ship in
the background. Our Captain at any rate looked rosy
and alive; his family were peaky and stiff, like dolls.
Rhoda came to business. Peter had seen it and said,

'It's a primitive. Primitives fetch a price.' And what was certain, he said, was that it would fetch three times as much if the Captain was sold with it.

'Rhoda! What a sad thing to do with a family thing. Sell the children? You don't mean it,' Miranda said.

Rhoda watched our faces.

'Well, I can tell you this – we're not selling the Captain, are we, Miranda?' I said. Let Rhoda sell what she liked. My temper was rising at the sight of Rhoda proposing to sell our things under our noses and turning our house into a saleroom. Rhoda went one better.

'I'll sell them to you if you like,' Rhoda said, dropping her mouth open like a haggler.

'We don't want them,' I said. 'Do we, Miranda?'

'But Rhoda, the two pictures are not by the same painter,' Miranda said. 'You can see that by the signatures. The children were done by some local man – Barnes or something. Ours is a Drummond.'

Rhoda was startled but shook the idea out of her head.

'Peter says it's a Drummond,' she argued.

'Soon settle that – look at the signature.'

It was illegible. On the back a label said: 'Flora Barnes. Falmouth.'

Miranda said shrewdly, 'Does Sammy want you to sell it?'

Rhoda put on an airy manner and gave one of her dry cackles. 'Sammy doesn't know I've got it here,' she said. 'He'd go out of his mind. I packed it up when he was at the club or with that woman of his.'

Her eyes went into slits of pleasure at the memory of her trick.

Miranda said, 'Have you left Sammy?'

'I'll never leave Sammy,' Rhoda said. 'And Sammy won't leave me. When he finds out I've got the picture and gets my letter about Peter and the prices things fetch he'll be over here on the next plane. Sammy will do anything for money. He'll bring the little boy.'

She went into a brisk dream.

'Gamblers love children and that woman hates them.'

'You mean and bring the – er – lady?'

Rhoda, Sammy, and his mistress on our doorstep!

'No,' said Rhoda. 'I don't mind what women he has, but he's had this one long enough. I know how to manage Sammy.'

Neither Miranda nor I could think of anything to say. Rhoda held out her glass and I gave her another drink. Rhoda saw that her proposal had failed and when her 'visions' fail, she always throws them away. She looked down at her shoes thoughtfully and said in her sly and deedy voice, very slowly sketching her way into a new idea: 'I actually don't think I will sell the picture when Sammy gets here. I haven't any children of my own. The boy is rather sweet. He likes the picture: he thinks they're mine.'

And then she said, shrewdly, 'Peter says when you go in for antiques it's always a good thing to have something you *won't* sell in a shop.'

And Rhoda knelt on the floor and began to put the picture back into its sacking. I helped her.

I said, 'I can't see Sammy in an antique shop. You can't sleep all day in a shop.'

'I'll run the shop,' she said. 'I'm going to talk to Peter tomorrow. He might come in with us. They'll get on – they're both keen on money – and he's younger than Sammy. That'll keep Sammy awake.'

We both shouted wih laughter and Rhoda was surprised for a moment and then looked very clever. She went to sit on the stool.

Miranda said that dinner was ready and as she went into the kitchen called back, 'Is Peter married, Rhoda?'

'God, no,' Rhoda called back, and looked at me suggesting that there was something stupid in our married condition.

We went to eat in the alcove at the end of the room. When we were served she put her head almost down to her plate and looked up to see what our forks were putting into our mouths before she began.

There was no more talk about pictures or Peter or Sammy, but we laughed about old times at Lodge – the soldiers there, how kind Captain Blake was to her the night Plymouth was bombed and how Miranda had found her sitting on the captain's knee in her nightgown and she had fallen asleep and had a terrible dream that she was struggling with Miranda in the sea.

Rhoda said, 'I thought you were drowned. I was trying to save you.'

Miranda said drily, 'And you brought me a cup of tea every morning for a week afterwards. I wondered why.'

'It was weird,' said Rhoda, ignoring this. 'Mother was so upset. I was only talking to poor Captain Blake. He was only being cuddly – he wasn't my lover, you know . . .'

'I should hope not. You were only a child,' said Miranda.

'He was after *you* – but *you* had Philip,' Rhoda said and turned to me and said, 'What was all the fuss about? Anyway, he told me he was impotent . . .'

'Shut up, Rhoda,' I said.

She looked mischievously at me but obeyed.

After this there was no more fuss until bedtime. Then she insisted on having her travelling-bed put up alongside the empty bed in the spare room, and when this was done she complained that it blocked the way to the window. She said she would sooner sleep on the floor in the sitting-room, so we let her bring her sleeping-bag down, and we helped her dismantle her travelling-bed. She said she wanted to slip away in the morning without disturbing us.

'I will say goodbye now. I'll be off at six o'clock. I never eat breakfast,' she said.

Then she wanted a needle and cotton to mend the lining of her beret, which – it turned out – was Sammy's.

So we left her and went up to our room. I said to Miranda, 'Sammy must be a saint to live with a woman like that.'

'She *does* worry me,' Miranda said. 'That dream of hers about struggling with me in the sea. Do you think I was beastly to her when she was a child? I do hope she's comfortable.'

I could not get to sleep until three in the morning. I looked out of the window: the light from the sitting-room still lit up the lawn. When I woke up about seven I had an alarming thought about the Trafalgar Captain. I went downstairs and was relieved to see he was still hanging on the wall. I went to the front door. Her car had gone but on the doorstep there was Granny's little stool propped up against the bootscraper. Had she thought of taking it? Had she forgotten or changed her mind?

Rhoda's voice buzzed in our ears in the next few days. She did not telephone or write. Months went by without news. I suppose we shall hear at Christmas. Miranda thinks Rhoda is like one or two of the old village people here who seem to be made of weather rather than flesh and blood. They live in their fancies and 'seeings', trying out their lives in the air, trying their feelings on the market, shrewdly watching the bidders.

'She was trying out herself and her ideas on us,' Miranda said. 'Crystal-gazing like a gypsy. Making up her mind about Sammy.'

I don't know. Six months after she left, that Peter Ogbourne fellow came to the house, touting for antiques, and I sent him away with a flea in his ear, but we did ask him about Rhoda.

'Very kind old lady,' he said politely. 'She gave me a lift to Plymouth.'

'I thought she was giving you a lift to Falmouth,' I said.

'The funny thing is I've never been to Falmouth in my life,' he said.

'She said something about showing you a picture of children – a Primitive,' I said.

'Not me. It must have been some other dealer. Or my father,' he said. 'But she did give me your address.'

A CHANGE
OF POLICY

Soon after six on a rainy London evening, when the
traffic was clogged and bleating in the streets, Paula got
back from Chelsea to her flat off Baker Street. She had
been reading to a learned old lady whose sight was
failing, a friend of her sister, and she was about to
change from her red dress – the one with the large gilt
buckle on it – when there was a long aggravating ring
at the doorbell. No doubt some stupid messenger had
mistaken her bell for that of the sportswear shop on the
ground floor. She went down the steep stairs and when
she opened the door there was the sharp back of a man
with greying hair who was shouting at a woman who
was trying to get her car into a parking place on the
other side of the street. He turned around.

'Hullo, Paula,' he said. 'Usual thing. Can't keep
my nose out of other people's troubles. That's a lie –
protecting my property. Don't want that silly woman
smashing into my car.'

Paula stared at him and, astonished, said, 'Mr Southey!'

'Same as the poet,' he said.

'George! I'm sorry, I didn't recognise you. Well, come in. You've grown a beard.'

As he followed her up the narrow staircase he said, 'I'm glad you noticed. A small Vandyke – keeping up with the lads at the works. Just got in from Munich – actually Istanbul.'

Paula's small sitting-room had tall windows and was made to look larger by a long discreet mirror that set off her height. A woman of taste: sets of small leatherbound books on the shelves on either side of the fireplace.

'Why didn't you telephone?' she said. She was easily irritated by people who dropped in. 'And *do* sit down.'

'I did,' he said. 'A message for me at the airport – from my brother – said the proofs of the *Quarterly* were two months late. I said, "That's not like Paula," saved time and went straight to the Prof Shop. No dice. They said you'd left, packed in the job, sent in your cards. Glowry gone, Featherstone too. New girl at reception.'

'Do sit down, George,' she said.

'I mean we've been printing the *Quarterly* for how long is it – years. What's going on?'

'I don't know,' she said. 'Yes, I did resign. I am not in touch with anyone there. There has been a change of policy.'

She wished he had not called the Institute 'the Prof

Shop'. It was a learned institution, a century old, inter-
nationally respected.

'But you ran the place,' said George. 'Arranged all
the foreign lectures, introduced them . . .'

'How did you know my address, George?' she asked.
She was a woman for rules, and there *was* a rule that
no private addresses could be given.

'That was easy,' he said. 'You've forgotten. I dropped
you and your sister here one night, five years ago.
After that lecture – Herr Doktor Wafflenbloater or
something, on the Catholic Church and the Third Reich.
You sneaked me in.'

'Dr Grein,' she said stiffly.

'There I go, flat on my face as usual. That's it –
Grein, of course. I call them all Wafflenbloater. You
introduced him, the only thing I understood. It was
pouring with rain, like tonight, and your sister and some
friend of his couldn't get a taxi afterward and I drove
you here, all of you. I remembered you said there was
an antique shop on the ground floor. I see it's a sports
shop now. Things change.'

'I remember now; you were very kind,' she said. 'She
was Dr Grein's wife, Sophie. And it is kind of you to
come now.'

'You told me not to drive too fast,' he said. 'Not kind
at all. Business is business. We're worrying about the
contract for the *Quarterly* – we've had it for years. What
do you mean you resigned? Did you storm out, or
what?'

He had known her well once, in the early days of the
Quarterly, when he used to bring in the proofs himself

and they went through them together. She had been a tall, calm, rather distant young woman with a quiet, clear, serious voice.

'You have changed your hair style,' he said. He remembered she had dark hair that had gravely framed her head. He had heard a lady sitting next to him at that Grein lecture say she looked exactly like George Eliot, whoever that was – very calm and certain. Now her hair was shorter, freer. It even looked chopped and wild.

'You've come to life,' he said. 'What are you doing?'

'Nothing.'

She really had 'stormed out'. She remembered it all: how the chairman had called her to his grand office, where he sat with the large Edwardian portrait of the founder of the Institute and the small one of the first committee, looking portentous on the grey wall behind him. The chairman said that the committee had decided that the Institute must be modernised. They intended to go for something called Communications, and they had put in a popular journalist to turn the *Quarterly* into a magazine, with newsy extracts from lectures instead of the full text. The new man had already brought in a young woman to run Personality Closeups.

George listened to her without expression. 'His mistress, I suppose,' he said.

'I have no idea,' she said in her principled voice. 'That could possibly have been a consideration.'

'So you stormed out?' he said.

'They didn't *fire* me, George,' she said. 'They wanted

me to run the library. The Old Folks Home, the Black
Hole of Calcutta, we used to call it. No one ever used
it. If they had asked me to go on the committee I would
have stayed. Yes, I suppose I stormed.'

She was remembering how on the afternoon when
she left the Institute a flight of pigeons clattered out of
the square near the British Museum and, it seemed to
her, flew the news of her angered virtue to those parts of
London where standards and integrity still had meaning.
She had influential, well-placed friends who had rallied
to her in London and in the country, when she went
there to stay. In those early weeks, she felt that she was
walking a yard or two above the earth. The trouble was
that her friends had outlived their influence; it had
leaked away. When you lose an important job, there
comes a time when there are silences: you embarrass,
you find yourself in a limbo, you become a curiosity.
Even the target of indignation loses its focus. After the
promising interviews that, one by one, came to nothing,
her story seemed to dissolve. Her money was running
out. This very day, as she came back on the crawling
bus from the old lady's flat, she had felt that the people
who were crowding into restaurants and shops and bars
or rushing along with parcels were employed. They had
homes, and soon, if nothing happened, she would be
forced to get out of hers.

'There was nothing personal in the reason for my
leaving,' she said, annoyed by any insinuation that
jealousy was at the heart of her decision.

He nodded. 'From our point of view, of course,' he
said, 'it doesn't matter what the Institute wants. We

print anything. That *Quarterly* gave us prestige. We took trouble with it. But if they want a comic, we can do it. If they want a colour magazine, we can do it. We print anything for anybody. Travel brochures, coloured wrappers, mottoes, anything from calendars to the Koran, printing for Eskimos, Malays, Arabs – we do a lot for Arabs. Even Old Masters, popular reproductions of the classy stuff. But why am I doing all the talking?'

'You do talk a lot, George,' she said, smiling at him. 'More than you used to in the old days, when you came in and we did the proofs.'

'That was because I couldn't make out what the *Quarterly* was about until you read out a sentence or some of those foreign names. What on earth are you doing reading to an old lady?' he said seriously. 'We've got to do something about that. I get ideas, you know. I run into a lot of people.'

The 'we' made her raise her fine eyebrows. She pointed to the typewriter on the table. She said she was doing some translation.

There he sat, not so much staring at her, she thought, as staring at himself in the tall mirror.

'You've changed,' she said. Working with him, she had taken him for granted as part of his trade. She had even felt she was, in some detached way, superior to him. But now, being in limbo, she began to see him as a man.

'As a matter of fact I have an offer to go to Kenya,' she said.

And it was true that the rich old lady had said to her in an erratic way, 'Why don't you come to Nairobi with me?' Clearly she didn't mean it; she was too old to move and was simply remembering her travels.

Why did I say that, Paula suddenly thought. I must be mad. She looked at his face. It was as set as a gambler's: he had drawn it out of her. She knew why she had talked. The virtue had gone out of her; the euphoria had disintegrated. If she could have got hold of that woman who had taken her job she would have slapped her face.

He seemed to know all this as he studied her.

'Derailed,' he said.

'I don't understand,' she said.

'Nothing. Old family saying. Didn't I tell you – my father worked in the shunting signal box at Euston when he started as a boy. First week, he put a truck of fish or something off the line. It upset him. He gave in his cards. Anyone loses their job in our family, like my sister's boyfriend not turning up on their wedding day, breaking the engagement – remind me to tell you about that – *derailed*, that's the word we use. I can hear him. Forget it – things come up in your mind.'

'You are ridiculous, George,' she said, and she laughed for the first time.

'It's true,' he said. 'That is what the old man used to tell us. Derailed. There it is.'

His excitement went. The flush went from his talking face and he stared at her. 'Come and have dinner with me,' he said.

'I can't,' she said. 'My sister will be here.'

'Bring her along. I remember her – she was with you when I picked you up after that meeting.'

Paula remembered her sister saying, 'Who was that awful little man – very kind, of course.' Just imagine it!

'Anyway, you've had a long flight. You must be exhausted. Your family is expecting you.'

'Oh, that's fixed,' he said. 'The boy's away at school.'

'But your wife . . .'

He looked at her steadily. 'No wife,' he said.

She waited for him to say more but he said nothing. He'd been married twice – he had told her. Separated? Surely he had not left that pretty, fair-haired girl who had worked in Reception and to whom they had all given a present when she married him? She remembered Featherstone, who was on the committee, saying in his disappointed way, 'I hope she doesn't regret it. The descendant of the poet is a bit of a rake.' But the laconic 'No wife' struck her as being a final refusal to speak.

'Don't you know?' he said.

'I don't know anything,' she said.

He had not been to the Institute more than once in the last two years. A young assistant had been sent in his place. She had supposed that was because he had become a partner in the firm, travelling about.

'If I may, I'd like to use your telephone to ring my son,' he said now. 'I always ring every day when I am away, to tell him where I am and when I'm getting back. I rang from Munich today – or yesterday – I've got the days all wrong. Boys worry. But they love long-distance telephone calls at school, it makes them feel important. I ring my wife first – I mean, I ring the hospital. My wife had a stroke nearly two years ago. She's at the Grafton Forster Hospital. She's been unconscious ever since. No change. She doesn't know who I am. No sign. I go and see her twice a week when I'm at home. Just lies there, eyes open. It happened when I was on the Australian trip. I came back at once.'

'George, why didn't you tell me? What a terrible story. I can't believe it . . . It must have been awful for you this time in Munich.'

'I had to go,' he said. 'You might as well be anywhere. I mean when you're nowhere . . .'

And she had been talking to him of the Institute, losing her job! Her limbo was petty compared with his.

He was totally transformed in her eyes. He was no longer the bouncing talker. That talk was hysteria. Even if she could not yet believe in the catastrophe, it had turned him from an actor into a human being who was himself. Even more terrible than the hospital visits were those daily telephone calls to the boy. She was ashamed of her own commonplace troubles.

And then her telephone rang. They both looked at the instrument on her desk.

'I gave the hospital this number,' he said. 'I always leave a number wherever I am. I'm a string of telephone numbers.'

She rushed to the telephone and answered it.

'Not for you,' she said, for George was on the edge of his chair. A man was talking.

She said dryly, 'You are a rare bird, aren't you? When did she let *you* out of the cage? No, I can't. I simply can't. Absolutely not. I have people here. Quite impossible.' And then she said, 'You should think of these things earlier.'

And then, rather grandly, glancing back at George she felt impelled to let George hear her telling a lie. It was like a confession. She seemed to grow taller.

'My sister and her husband are here, staying with me. We're going out to dinner. No, not tomorrow, I shall be in the country.' And putting down the receiver she looked angrily at it and said, 'I'm sorry.' She was blushing.

He was looking with admiration at her. 'I remember you at the Institute like that,' he said. 'Now you will have to say you will come to dinner with me. I have an idea. No need to go to Kenya. I know a Greek restaurant. We'll have to cross two parks to get there. It's a good place. Noisy. Full of young people. That means you can't hear what anybody is saying and they can't hear you. Very private. Real clatter.'

He got up and put out his hand to pull her up.

'All right,' she said, and, surprised, she let him pull her up. 'I am sure this is very bad for you. I'll just change into something.'

'May I telephone? The boy,' he said.

In the days when he used to come to the Institute she remembered she had seen him going off with one or the other of the girls at the reception desk of the office. Now, she thought as she went upstairs, he is not *that* man. She changed into a silk blouse that had a pattern of large green and blue leaves.

'Is this all right?' she asked when she returned.

'Just the job,' he said.

'Now,' she said when she was in his car and they drove out of her street, 'what was the news?'

'No change,' he said.

'The boy?' she said. 'Was he all right? What did he say? You didn't tell me his name.'

'Night jungle,' he said as they drove away, waving at the park. 'Rainy season. His name's Harry. The bother with boys is they're always asking questions. Mania for details.'

'I've got nephews,' she said.

'I had to go over the whole flight home. Change at Frankfurt – he never lets me miss out a change of plane. Wanted to know if I had seen any snakes in Munich. Mixing it up with when I came home from Australia two years ago. He's got snakes on his brain. Cobras or mambas. I cheated and said there was a dancing snake in the Munich Zoo that ends up hanging from the tree in a figure of eight. Actually, I think that's true,' he said. 'Now he's taken to horses, and I've taken up riding.'

He leaned forward, peering ahead as a traffic light changed. 'We'll skip Baker Street,' he said knowingly, 'and take a right. Fantastic dream.'

In the side streets she saw he was one of those drivers who cannot resist a sharp turn or a shortcut. Some passing motorist hooted at him.

'Now what did he mean by that?' he said.

'Your driving,' Paula said. 'You're not on a horse.'

Between a warehouse and a house with corrugated iron covering its windows was a door with a travel poster saying 'Come to Greece'. They had arrived.

He helped her out of the car, holding her arm. 'Mind you don't fall down the step.'

Noisy! She found herself ducking and going head first into a Greek song that swirled over her in the hot upper air. There was the sound of the open steaming kitchen, the open grill behind the distant counter, and, on either side of the narrow, pretty room, pairs of customers, most of them young. The youngest girls, bunch up in their jerseys and anoraks, were smiling and soundlessly talking.

'How comic,' she said. 'What is the song? Do you understand?'

'Not a word,' he said. 'It's probably about love, death, and goats.'

The young proprietor came up to him and said, 'Mr Southey,' and then murmured quietly, 'Any news?'

George shook his head. The proprietor raised his deploring hands.

In the middle of their meal George said, seriously, 'We've had a lot of bother in Munich. The Germans are very stubborn. We're doing a book on the Rubens in the old Pinakotek. The British publishers hate the translation. There's an idea – why don't you do it? Drop Kenya. You talk German. Come with me. You'll flabbergast them. Three or four days – call it five. There you are – a job. I'm serious. I'll see to it that my brother pays you decently. All expenses paid, of course – actually, it'll only take a couple of days. You can go to the Alps, see your old friends – the Greins and so on.'

'George, you are very kind. I'm very sorry, I could not possibly go there. I hate the place.'

'But you were there for two years. It's a fine city. You taught at the university.'

'No,' she said. 'I was *at* the university, but I taught at a school there. I was never so unhappy in my life. I never want to see the place again. I'm superstitious.'

The four men who were talking loudly near the counter suddenly shouted with laughter and two of them punched each other and went on laughing. She frowned at the noise. She felt it was splitting her in two and that part of herself was being dragged back into the past, and that George was not the person she could possibly tell about it.

'I see,' he said.

The two neutral words began to exasperate her because they were neutral. That 'I see' had turned him into a stranger. She ought to have turned him down flat. She had gone too far. And then her feeling changed. She thought of him making those calls to the hospital and to his son every day: he had not hidden his misery. The noise, the songs howling out their imaginary passions, all the more forceful for being meaningless, undermined her reserve.

'As I expect you know,' she said, '*I* nearly married a German.'

She waited for him to say 'Yes, I know.'

'I didn't know that,' he said. 'I don't know anything about you.'

'I thought perhaps you did,' she said.

'If I had I wouldn't have mentioned it.'

'Dr Grein,' she said.

'Waffen – Sorry – Grein! You mean the man who gave that lecture when I drove you and your sister home? Well, there I go, flat on my face again.'

'It was over then. He came with his wife. I was in love with him before he married, but it went wrong. There is no reason why I shouldn't tell you this, except you said your first wife was a German and a Catholic. Dr Grein's a Catholic.'

'You mean he wouldn't divorce his wife?' he said. 'You can if you know the ropes.'

The ropes!

'I was very young. People broke it up: his family, my sister.'

'Religion is a curse,' he said. 'I've seen too much of it. What it does to people.'

'That is simply not *true*,' she said sharply in her correcting way. 'My sister is a deeply religious woman. She objected because Heinrich's family were peasants. I'd written to my father and told him this. She read the letter to him. She sent me a telegram saying my father was very ill. I went home at once. He was going blind. I used to read to him. It went on for a month. I always seem to be reading to blind people! My father kept saying, "Where's this man? I want to have a look at him." But Heinrich didn't come. His father and mother were sweet, simple people. They were nice to me, but when I was away they warned him against me. All the little hill farms there look like children's toys, all the villages, too, so clean and bright, the fields so green climbing up to pinewoods, and after that the rock and the snow, the air so pure. It turned my head, I suppose.'

'There's nothing toylike about peasants,' he said. 'They're not children.'

'I know,' she said. 'I never want to see the place

again. Thank you for asking me, if you really meant it.'

'Oh, well,' he said. 'My brother can settle it. Really, there's no need for anyone to go. The firm can do the job just as well in London.'

'That's much better, George,' she said. 'With all this worry about your wife it would be madness to go back to Munich. If I were in your position I would be thinking all the time, "Suppose she wakes up, suppose she dies." You've got back today, but every day you were away must have been awful.'

He said, looking like stone, 'I'm "away" here in London. I've been "away" for almost two years. I'm nowhere.'

'You're not really away, George. You take your love for your wife and your son with you everywhere.'

He sat back from the table as if to make himself distant and said, quietly, under the noise of the place, 'I didn't come to see you about the proofs. I came to see *you*. You are very beautiful. I want you.'

She could not stop the freezing lines of horror forming on her face – not at what he had said but horror of herself. She sat back looking nervously at the people in the restaurant, and in confusion she said, 'I'm not beautiful. I didn't think . . . I never thought . . . George, you must see – but thank you, George, please don't go on with this. I don't go in for that sort of thing. Even if I felt – You must see, I would not do that to your wife. Don't be angry. Any woman likes to hear it. I admire you, George, but I don't like messes. I couldn't – Oh damn, don't look so hurt, George. I envy your wife. She is a very lucky woman to be loved as you love her. I'm not a prude. I don't mean you are wrong. I mean that it would be wrong for me.'

'I see,' he said in his flat, maddening way and simply stared.

She said, looking down at her empty coffee cup with suppressed anger, 'It's natural. You want a woman.' And she looked up at him.

'You,' he said. 'I always have.'

'I don't like bedroom affairs,' she said, and suddenly burned with jealousy of George's wife, indeed of all the women in the restaurant. She could hear her sister saying, 'What is the matter with you? Why do you keep falling for impossible men?'

'Can we go?' she said.

He called for the bill. There was another loud shout of laughter from the men at the table in the corner of the bar and one of them reached for another bottle of wine.

The proprietor himself brought the bill, and after George paid it they got up and the proprietor followed them to the door. He said to George, 'I hope you have good news.' And to her, 'Thank you, my lady, and be careful of the step.'

They were out in the rainy drizzle and got into the car. He said, 'I've spoiled the evening. I'm sorry.'

Whatever was in her head, her body hated him to say that.

'You have a right to ask me. Everyone has a right.'

'Like the man who rang you at your flat?' he said.

'That was just an old friend,' she said sharply. Damn again: he had noticed that.

They drove back through the two parks, empty jungles, under the artificial pink city sky. They did not speak. It was awful that the talker did not speak. When he stopped outside her house she said, 'Thank you for dinner, George. You must get some sleep.'

'Sleep?' he said. 'I've the feeling that I've been standing up all night for years.'

Then he pointed. 'The usual London cat on your doorstep,' he said. 'Not yours?'

She got out and said 'Shoo' to the cat and then, 'You do promise to tell me, please, if there is good news. I'll pray for it.'

'Pray?' he said.

She watched the tail-light of his car getting smaller and smaller as he drove away down the street. It seemed to her that, like him, she had been standing up all night. He had not even said he loved her, thank heavens. Since Grein's time she had not loved any of her one or two lovers. She shivered at the appalling simplicity of George's situation.

The next day she was glad to go to read to the old lady.

'Something has happened to you,' the old lady said. 'I can tell by your voice. You have good news.'

The lines of the old lady's face lit up with conspiratorial pleasure. Paula was surprised at hearing herself say she had been offered an interpreting job in Munich but only for a few days.

The old lady said 'Munich!' and talked of the time she and her husband and a friend called Tregarron had been there before the war. The old lady scowled at a memory as she went on and then suddenly stopped. There was something like a harsh call to arms in the confused ruined corridors of the old lady's mind. She said sharply, 'That was where your silly sister had that stupid affair with some Nazi professor when she was at the University. Grein or something. Laborious fellow – common. You and your father had to go there and get her out of it.'

'Dr Grein was not a Nazi,' said Paula loudly. 'My sister did not have an affair with him. Who told you that? Professor Grein is a very distinguished, happily married man. You must be thinking of someone else. My sister would never do anything like that.'

The old lady was frightened. She offered Paula a piece of marzipan.

'Now, when are you going to Kenya?' Paula asked to distract her.

'Who told you I was going to Kenya?' asked the old lady.

'You did,' Paula said. 'You said you had a friend down there.'

A tear ran down the old lady's face. 'I have no friends,' she said. 'All my friends are dead. You are my only friend.'

I ought to have gone to see George's poor wife in hospital and stop wasting my time with old friends of my sister, Paula said to herself when she got back to her flat. Why didn't anyone at the Institute tell me that this had happened to the girl? It's the least I can do for that man. Such a pretty girl. She had always felt protective of those 'children', as she called the typists at the Institute. Perhaps the sight of someone she had known in the past would have the curing effect of shock.

Two days later, she put down her work and with mission in her eyes she took the train from London to the Sussex town. She felt exalted watching the green country wheel wider and wider as the train cut through it. But when the train gave out its electric howl as it rushed into the peremptory tunnel under the Downs and emerged at the station of the town, she suddenly thought, How awful of me. I ought to have asked George. What an intrusion. How awful if I met him in the street.

The town was bunched on a steep hill of confusing little streets. Halfway up the hill, the traffic was heavy as buses and trucks rumbled past to the coast. She remembered George telling her that the place was famous for its murder trials at the county court and its religious riots. One year, the Pope had been burned in effigy on Guy Fawkes Day, and George had made her laugh with the tale of a woman from the marshes who was known to stick pins into a doll on the window of her cottage and to shout 'Curse his name! Curse his name!' as she did it.

At last she got to the long red brick hospital and its car park. She gave the name of the patient she wanted to see to the clerk at the entrance and found herself in the waiting room sitting with a dozen other visitors, all silent, all staring at the door as they had done at the sight of her. We look like a coven of witches, she thought. She had imagined that she would have been taken immediately to the Sister and certainly the doctor. She sat there thinking of what she would say when she would be taken to see the patient. Someone said, 'The doctor's doing the wards,' and half an hour passed before her name was called. When she was led to the ward she asked, foolishly, 'May I speak to her?'

'Of course. The others do. She won't answer.'

'We used to work in the same office. She was my secretary,' said Paula humbly to the down-to-earth sister who joined them for a moment as they stood looking at the now grey-haired woman lying unmoving, her eyes open. There was a sudden crash of oxygen cylinders that were being unloaded from a truck in the yard outside. The eyes did not move.

Suddenly it occurred to Paula to speak in a peremptory office voice: 'Ethel!' she said. 'The moment Mr Southey gets here, tell him that I have a message from your son Harry. Please bring him to my room at once.'

There was no movement of the eyes.

The Sister said, 'Mr Southey has been this morning. If he's away he always telephones.'

Once more there was the crash of the oxygen cylinders.

'Mr Southey's brother and his wife always call.'

As Paula left the hospital she saw new people in the waiting room. They seemed to be trying to read her face as she hurried to the door. She glanced at the marshes stretching to the foot of the Downs as she hurried back to the station. She wondered where George lived in the town. She went up to the end of the platform to be away from the other passengers waiting for the next train. It was market day in the town and she could hear the calves lowing in their pens. Then, sparkling with electric flashes, the plain yellow-faced London train came in. Not until it had taken her out through that dramatic short tunnel that seemed to her to pass under the hospital did she feel free and unwatched. Under the spell of the racing train, as the countryside circled and the bridges seemed to shout at her, and branch lines swerved away into places unknown to her, and the living sky seemed to ride with her, did she think, Why did I do that presumptuous, untruthful thing?'

At last the train slowed down and rumbled over the Thames and squealed as it slowly turned into the terminus, and, released, she got up from her seat and joined the crowd that rushed to the barrier and, once past it, scattered with intent in their eyes. She threw away her usual prudence about money and took a taxi to her house. There she stood in her sitting-room, among her things, and looked at the assuring, demure white houses opposite, and then went up to her bedroom and changed her clothes and washed her hands and did her face and went down to her desk and telephoned to George and waited impatiently while a secretary went to look for him. At last he answered. 'Trouble with a machine,' he said.

'I hope you don't mind, George. I went down to the hospital this morning to see Ethel. I hope you don't think I was intrusive.'

'So the nurse said,' he said. His voice was dull. 'It was kind of you.'

'Not kind. It was terrible. George, I've just got back home.' And then, in a quieter voice, 'I think I have good news for you.'

'You've got a job?'

'No, no, George,' she said impatiently. 'You remember – what you were saying? When are you coming to London? We could talk. Not on the phone, not today. My sister is coming. Tomorrow, George. I can't tell you now.'

Soon the Hoover was howling in the flat. Her sister did not come.

On the Saturday evening, up the stairs he came, into the room. She sat on one of the small armchairs and he on the sofa, staring at her. In the small room the literal distance between them seemed to him to be enormous and to her puzzling. She had planned that he would be sitting on the chair and she would prop herself on the sofa; they were wrongly placed.

'George,' she said. 'I will.'

He stared at her and she said, 'I'm shy. Why don't you kiss me, George?'

He jumped up and went to her and was astonished that she turned her head this way and that to keep him away, so that they almost wrestled.

'We shall be on the floor,' she said with a laugh so harsh that he let her go.

'Not here,' she said, clutching his hand. 'Upstairs.'

She laughed as she pulled him up the stairs and then looked at him with a gloating defiant stare as she pulled off her clothes and he followed her to the bed.

'Printer!' she laughed. 'You are a snake. What are you doing here?'

Then, 'How thin you are.'

Then, 'How strong,' and she groaned, 'Go on, go on – you're killing me.' And then softly, 'Oh, darling,' and her eyes flooded with tears of pleasure. 'No more,' she said.

They lay in silence for a long time.

'When did you first think of me?' she asked.

'When I first saw you,' he said.

'That was years ago,' she said.

'When did you?' he said.

'I don't know – when you asked me.'

'Not before that?' he said.

'I think when you told me about ringing your son – I don't know,' she laughed. 'When you grew a beard, Mr Vandyke.'

And that was not the end of it. In the morning he was still asleep, with his mouth open. She smiled at that and kissed him on the forehead, but he did not move. She gathered her clothes together and went to the bathroom. The sound of running water did not disturb him. After a while he called. There was no answer. He slept again. And then there she was in the room, astonishingly wearing a hat and a light coat and carrying a handbag.

'Where are you going?' he said.

'Nowhere. I've just come back from church. Get up.'

'Church!' he said, astonished. 'To confession?' he mocked.

'Of course not,' she said sharply. 'I always go. I told

you my father was a clergyman. I went to pray for your wife,' she said gravely. 'Have you rung the hospital?'

'Yes, I did when I woke up,' he said bluntly. 'Nothing.'

She wanted to rush at him and to kiss him, and not till they were eating breakfast at a little table in the living room did he say, 'It was lovely,' and she put her hand out to him and he kissed it.

'When are you going to ring your son?' she asked.

'Not on Sunday mornings. They're at church. I go riding. I'll get him at teatime.'

And he went on to explain that on Sundays his cleaning woman did not come and he had lunch at the hotel or at his brother's. 'When the Germans come over with the Munich book you must come down to the works. You must meet my brother, see my house.'

She interrupted sharply. 'You must understand, G, I could not possibly do *that*,' she said firmly.

They went to the park, where the sky was wide and open. There was a distant bellowing and screeching of animals from the zoo as they passed the absurd cricket matches and the couples clinging on the grass, the girls pulling down their dresses to their knees, and the older couples calling their dogs that raced away in wider and wider circles. A man was teaching his son to fly a kite; it twirled around and somersaulted again and again until at last it flew up high and twirled again and dived fast to the ground.

'My son is getting too old for kites. He wants an aeroplane,' George said.

They walked to the long lake where old ladies and

children were feeding the ducks, and they laughed at the noisy parties in the rowing boats.

'I'm hungry,' she said. 'There's not much to eat in these cafés on Sundays.'

They went to a crowded place outside the park, and the day dawdled as he drove back to her flat.

'No,' she said. 'You're mad, George,' but he gripped her hand and they went upstairs.

The dark had come as she watched the red light of his car vanishing down the street.

She felt in their walk through the park that she belonged to the real world now and that George had renewed her life and that she was part of things that lived, the growing trees, even the grass, the birds flying over, even dogs racing, the children and every person she passed – even the people, unknown to her, who lived in the distant houses that surrounded the park, even people in the sky, as an occasional aeroplane passed across it, flying to the east, the west, the north, or the south. And, mysteriously, she felt at one with his wife and his son. Now she worked with heightened alacrity on the book she was translating; she loved seeing the German words turned into English, as if she were giving new birth to them. She was becoming useful again after that long period when she had left the Institute. Her anger had gone. She was needed.

George brought the news that two Germans from the firm publishing the Munich book were coming to his brother's works for the day and George wanted her to go down there to interpret. George's son would be there, too; it was the time of the boy's half-term holiday. George brought him to the station to meet her as she arrived. 'Here's Harry,' he said.

She saw a plump boy with reddish hair who stared at her defiantly when they shook hands.

'My mother is in hospital,' he said. 'She can't talk.'

'I know,' she said. 'I am very sorry. She and I used to work in the same office.'

'Dad said,' he said. 'Are you a German?'

'Oh no,' she said. 'But I speak German. That is why I have come.'

They went to the works. There was George's brother wearing a white dust coat. Two Germans stiffly bowed. The boy followed them round as they looked at the machines and listened to her speaking English and then German. He was awed by her, and whenever she spoke he moved his lips trying to copy her, saying the strange words. At last, since no one paid attention to him, he began quietly mocking her, saying, 'Vee fill, gobble, high Slosh, goramma de goramma, nine ten, volly gelob, Ya, Ya.'

'Shut up,' his father said.

So the boy followed them muttering. He hated her, and when they all went to look at a line of damp prints hanging on a line he gave her a sly kick on the shin. She glanced at him and said nothing. He was about to give her another kick when his father said, 'Stop that or you go home.' The boy was frightened and now followed her slowly.

'Your father says you have got a grass snake,' she said. 'Where do you keep it? Will you show it to me?'

142

'Ah,' said the younger of the Germans. '*Eine Ringel-natter*. Where is it?'

After that the boy was quiet, and he dropped out of the procession. When the visit was over, she went to the boy and asked, 'Where *is* your snake? Show it to me. What is its name?'

'Snakey,' he said.

The party walked to his uncle's house and the boy ran into the garden and came back with the snake, which had wound itself round his arm. A triumph.

'Oh, don't let it come near me!' Paula called out. 'It'll sting me.'

'It doesn't sting.'

The Germans laughed. Everyone laughed.

'Stroke it,' said the boy.

She touched it. 'Oh, it's cold!' she said.

The boy jumped about.

'Calm down,' said George. 'I think it wants to be in its box.'

'Come on. I'll show you where I keep it in the garden,' said the boy.

'Next time,' said his uncle, looking at his watch. 'We've got to get to Brighton for lunch. You've been very helpful,' he said to Paula. 'Why are you limping?'

'Oh, that,' she said. 'I knocked my shin against that machine.'

And so they went off to Brighton, over the Downs, to shouts of '*Wunderbar!*' and jokes about the British Alps without any *Schnee*, and at last to the first sight of the sea flying out like a flag, and to lunch with speeches from the two Germans, and jokes about the esteemed lady, and glasses clinking and bows in all directions. They said how they would all meet in Frankfurt in a month's time – or was it a week's time? And when it was over and George was going to drive them to Gatwick airport, she begged him to put her on the train because her leg was painful.

'You'd better stay here. I'll get a room,' he said.

'Darling George,' she said. 'I can't. I'm exhausted. Drop me at the station. I must get back to London. Don't look so sad, George.'

'Trains every half hour,' he said. And he drove by a longer route on the outskirts of the town, passing a church in a long village street.

'Church,' he said, jerking his thumb. 'See that? Parson coming out – see that? Kids riding ponies. Cricket field at the back. Nice place to retire to.'

And then, after a steep climb, he got her to the station barrier, and there in the clanging of luggage trolleys she said, 'I loved seeing Harry. He's like you.' And she tapped him on the chest. 'When do you go to Frankfurt?'

He pulled out his diary and said, 'Ten days' time.'

She snatched it from him and, looking at it, said, 'All those "X"s. Who's that?'

'You,' he said. 'Let's get onto the platform.'

'No,' she said. 'I hate platform goodbyes.'

Five days later he rang her and was at her door in the afternoon. The trip to Frankfurt had been brought forward.

'It's tomorrow,' he said. 'Change your mind and come with me.'

'I can't possibly come. I've invited my sister,' she said. 'She'll be here while you're away. You are annoying, G.'

He looked at the small pile of typescript on her table and at the page that was sticking out of her typewriter and then at the open German book. 'Well, if you can't come, read some to me,' he said suddenly. 'I want to hear you speak it, like when the Germans were here, and then I'll think of it all the bloody week while I'm away. Anything, just to hear your beautiful voice.'

'G, how strange you are today.'

In the end she agreed and picked up the book, opened it at random, and read.

'A bit more,' he said.

So she read on and then laughed at him. 'You didn't understand a word.'

'I did. *Frauen* something.'

'*Frauenkirche*,' she said.

He said, 'That's it. The way your throat moved. Say it again.' And then he had his arm around her and she was struggling against him.

'You were thinking of your pretty German wife,' she said, and she struggled until she was helpless, as she had been that first time. 'Not here, George,' she said. 'No, not on the floor.'

And when she got up from it she said, 'Tell your son you're the snake. The German is *Schlange*.'

The next day he left for Frankfurt.

'Ring me when you get there!' she called after him.

145

'You bet,' he said.

She worked all day and that evening he rang her. 'It's hell,' he said. 'You'd hate it. Hundreds of publishers sniffing round one another like dogs. Chinese, Japanese, American, half Europe, all the disunited nations. How many pages have you done?'

'You love it, you old fraud,' she said. 'Have you rung the boy?'

'Yes,' he said.

The next evening he rang again, and the next day, he said there was going to be a trip down the Rhine.

On the third day he said he was calling to ask how many pages she had done. 'It's calming down here,' he said. 'Tomorrow there's going to be some excursion. I don't know where – to some wine place. No, wait a minute – that's the day after tomorrow. By the way, our German friends, especially the big one – you remember – want to be remembered to you. I think he's going to send you a present. I wonder what. How many pages?'

On the fourth day there was no call and she rang the hotel and someone said he was out at the museum, not in his room, and someone else said, 'Not at the museum, on the excursion.' There was a gabble of voices on the hotel exchange, and after a long time she heard a man who said he was the manager and asked who was speaking and she said, in German, 'I simply want to speak to Doctor Southey, with the British delegation, who is staying with you. It's urgent.' And she said vehemently, 'This is his wife, speaking from London.'

And she heard the man say to someone, 'You fool, why didn't you tell me this lady was his wife?' And she could clearly hear him say, 'You rang his brother? Where is his brother, at the hospital?'

She was trapped in a net of angry voices. And then the manager spoke again: 'Madame, we have supposed his brother must have told you. You must prepare yourself for bad news. I assure you we got in touch with his office at once. We supposed his brother would have passed the knowledge to you. Doctor Southey died in hospital yesterday, after a riding accident.'

'Get off the line!' she shouted. 'I am speaking to someone.'

The manager repeated his sentence. 'Not deaf,' he shouted. 'Dead. *Tod. Doktor Southey ist gestorben.*' And he repeated one of his long, riddlelike sentences.

Paula felt her face collapse. The strength went out of her hands and out of every object in the room, and indeed her whole body seemed to be jumping away from her and leaving her. She dropped the telephone, which hung squawking on its cord.

'George, you conceited fool –' she began.

'Stop that!' she shouted at the telephone.

She felt her body shrinking to nothing and then suddenly grossly bursting, as if to mock her. She seemed to hear George say those words that always annoyed her when he was caught out and was trying to smooth his way out of something – words that now grew fainter and fainter: 'There I go, flat on my face.'

'George, why didn't you tell me?' she whispered as if she were looking for him in the room.

And then the news became real to her. 'That poor boy,' she said. And now she did believe the news. 'His poor wife,' she said. 'This will kill her.'

She felt that half her life had been ripped out of her, that she was hanging in suspense between the present and her earlier memories of him, which became more vivid and real than the recent ones. Almost cautiously, she went from room to room, not able to believe that he would never again be sitting on that chair or this, or walk up the stairs. And then she could hear him making those telephone calls to the hospital and to his son at school.

Some days later a formal card announcing the memorial service arrived, saying 'Funeral Private.' With it there was a short typed letter from George's brother thanking Paula for her beautiful letter and the lovely wreath. Paula had also sent her love to the boy, and from him in time there came a letter written on lined paper from his school:

Dear Mrs Paula. I hope you are quit well. A beastly dog got Snakey. I have got a new one.

A few years ago two new London ladies became noticeable in the village of X. They settled in a cottage near the church at the top of the long street and walked every day to the post office in the afternoons. In fact, only the tall gaunt one with the thick grey hair who takes long steps is, strictly speaking, a Londoner. The little one with the reddish dyed hair is well known to be the sister-in-law of the printer who lives two miles away on the outskirts of the town. She trots along with a scraping step, chattering to the tall one, who, when they first came to live there, was thought to be a nurse, for it was known that the little one had been for a long time in the hospital in the town, lying there in a coma for goodness knows how long, after a stroke. About that, she has nothing to say, of course, for that part of her life is missing, but what she does not fail to say, with pride, too, about herself and the tall one called Paula is that they had been friends since they worked in the same office in London, at a place called the Institute.

'When we were girls,' she says. 'That is where I met my husband.'

Her husband is buried in the new plot of land the church had taken over some years back: a man said to have been in his time a fast bowler in the village cricket team.

About Paula, the tall one, little is known beyond the fact that once or twice a week she drives in a small car to the university ten miles away. Three or four of the village people even went to a lecture she gave on some German subject at the Literary Society in the town. There was a poster on the door of the Village Hall, and the daughter of the woman who runs the post office and village shop and has a big black dog went to the lecture. And so, indeed, did the printer and his wife. The village also knows that it is Ethel's, the little one's, son who comes down at weekends. He is a good-looking young man who often goes for a walk up on the Downs with

Paula. His mother goes only as far as the footpath at the end of the village because she can't manage the steep climb.

Their cottage is really two small flint-and-tiled cottages turned ingeniously into one. Ethel has a room on the ground floor, with a door giving onto the long lawn because she finds stairs tiring. Paula works in a room upstairs, where one wall is lined with books, and she sleeps in a narrow room that looks out onto the churchyard. Behind the house is a public footpath and a handsome row of sycamores and then the cricket field and the pink villas of the newer part of the village. In the afternoons and some evenings the two ladies sit in a sitting room, which is almost luxurious, for it is furnished with one or two treasures Paula brought down from her London flat there. There is a long, tall gilded mirror on one wall, a *chaise-longue*, and a cabinet with one or two pieces of china in it. The chairs are pleasantly low-seated, the windows are long and look out across the garden hedge to the public footpath, and it is pleasant to hear the gate slamming at the end of it and to see who has gone by.

Quite a number of distinguished visitors come to the house, especially one or two professors from Paula's university, and this is the time for Ethel to show her gift of bringing in large glasses, like globes, containing her speciality: well-iced and powerful gin-and-vermouths. When she comes into the room she always catches the ends of the sentences she hears and repeats them as if to give the impression that she had not been out of the room. If she hears a visitor saying 'In my opinion the film is a disaster to anyone who has read the book,' she glides in saying, '– To anyone who has read the book,' to join in the conversation. When her son is there and perhaps says, 'It was three-one at halftime,' she will eagerly repeat, 'Three-one at half-time.' She is making up for the time she was in hospital for all those years and heard nothing. She is particularly quick to pick up Paula's exclamations in the garden when Paula finds a climbing rose has gone wild and says, 'Nothing to be done with them. Cut them back or they go on, regardless with ideas of their own.' Ethel says, with fervour, '– With ideas of their own.' When someone says, 'Munich has the finest collection of pictures in Europe,' she repeats, 'the finest in Europe,' as if she had been visiting there all her life.

Ethel's son has turned into a plump and dressy young man with the habit of making a hissing noise between his teeth when he is bored. On Saturdays there is sometimes a sharp bang, like a shot, from the gate to the footpath at the side of the house. The gate slams loudest when the children from the pony club ride through.

'I wish that woman from the riding school would take her horses some other way,' says Paula.

'– Her horses some other way,' says Mrs Southey as she limps into the room. She adds, 'The noise interferes with Paula's work. How can she concentrate?'

But both women are thinking of George's death. His widow says, 'It was all conceit. I could understand if he had had a woman – but a horse! I'm not being funny.'

And she rambles into memories of the Institute and

says to Paula, 'Everyone thought you were going to marry Mr Featherstone. He made sheep's eyes at everyone. You don't know the whole of it.'

Her son listens. He would sooner be down at the village pub but he knows the ladies expect him to take them out to dinner on Saturdays at some restaurant or other. He likes his food and always wants to try a new place.

'Where shall we go?' Paula asks.

He pulls out his diary and looks down a list of telephone numbers.

'All those telephone numbers – just like George,' Paula says.

'I collect them,' he says. 'I started when I was at school. Dad used to ring me up from all over Europe.'

'Yes,' says Mrs Southey primly. 'We've got all his diaries, with numbers from all over the world.'

The shabby diaries are a guide to George's life when she was absent from it.

'He even telephoned from Turkey,' the young man said.

'And,' said Paula, 'sometimes from my house to the hospital and to your school.'

'Yes, you told me,' said Ethel, pitying her. 'He had no regard for anyone's convenience.'

THE
IMAGE
TRADE

What do you make of the famous Zut – I mean his stuff in this exhibition? Is he just a newsy collector of human instances jellied in his darkroom, or is he an artist – a Zurbarán, say, a priest searching another priest's soul? Pearson, one of a crowd of persons, was silently putting these questions to them on a London bus going north.

Last July, Pearson went on, he was at home. The front-door bell rang. 'He's here! On time!' his beautiful wife said. She was scraping the remains of his hair across his scalp. 'Wait,' she said, and turning him round, she gave a last sharp brush to his shoulders and sent him dibble-dabbing fast down three flights of stairs to the door. There stood Zut, the photographer, with his back to Pearson and on impatient feet, tall and thin in a suit creased by years of air travel. He was shouting to Mrs Zut, who was lugging two heavy bags of apparatus up the street to the house. She got there and they turned round.

As a writer, in the news too and in another branch of the human-image trade, Pearson depended on seeing people and things as strictly they are not. The notion that Zut and his wife could be a doorstep couple offering to buy old spectacles or discarded false teeth, a London trade, occurred to him, but he recovered and, switching on an eager smile, bowed them into the house. They marched past him down the hall, briskly, like a pair of surgeons, to the foot of the stairs and looked back at him.

'I hope you had no difficulty in finding this – er – place,' Pearson said, vain of difficulty as a sort of fame.

'None,' said Zut. 'She drives. I read the street map.' Mrs Zut had not put down her load. Zut seemed to ask, Are you the body?

Well, said Pearson spaciously, where did they want to 'do', or 'take' – he hesitated between saying 'it' or 'me'. He said this to all photographers, waving a hand, offering the house. Zut looked up at the stairs and the high ceiling.

Pearson said, Ground-floor dining room, tall windows, books? Upstairs by half-landing, a balcony, or would you say patio, flowers, shrubs, greenery, a pair of Chinese dogs in stone, view of neighbouring gardens? Down below, garden seat under tree, could sit there taking the air. And talking of air, have often been done – if that is the word – outside in the street, in overcoat and fur hat by interesting railings, coat buttoned or unbuttoned. No? Or first-floor sitting room. High windows again, fourteen feet in fact, expensive when curtaining, but chairs easy or uneasy, large mirror, peacock feathers on wife's desk, quite a lot of gilt, *chaise-longue* indeed. Have often been done there, upright or lying full length. *Death of Chatterton* style.

Zut said, 'Furniture tells me nothing. Where do you work?'

'Work?' said Pearson.

'Where you write,' said Zut.

'Oh, that,' said Pearson. 'You mean the alphabet, sentences? At the top. Three flights up, I'm afraid,' apologising to Mrs Zut. (Writer, writing at desk, rather a cliché for a man like Zut – no?)

Already Zut was taking long steps up the stairs, followed by Mrs Zut, who refused to give up her two rattling bags, Pearson looking at Mrs Zut's grey hair and peaceful back as he came after them. From flight to flight they went and did not speak until they were under a fanlight at the top. In a pause for breath Pearson said, 'Burglar's entry.'

Zut ignored this and, pointing to a door, 'In here?' he said.

'No, used to be children's bathroom. Other door.' The door was white on the outside, yellowing on the inside. They marched in.

'It smells of – what would you say? – decaying rhubarb, I'm afraid. I smoke a pipe.'

There was the glitter of permafrost in Zut's hunting eyes as he studied the room. There were two attic windows; the other three walls were blood red but stacked and stuffed with books to the ceiling. They were terraced like a football crowd, in varieties of anoraks, a crowd unstirred by a slow game going on among four tables where more books and manuscripts were in scrimmage.

'That your desk?' said Zut, pointing to the largest table.

'I'm a table man,' said Pearson, apologising, bending to pick up one or two matches and a paper clip from the floor. 'I migrate from table to table.' And drew attention to a large capsized photograph of the Albert Memorial propped on a chest of drawers. Accidentally, Zut kicked a metal wastepaper basket as he looked round. It gave a knell.

Yes, Pearson was inclined to say (but did not), this room has a knell. Authors die. Dozens of funerals of unfinished sentences here every day. It is less a study than a – what shall I say? – perhaps a dockyard for damaged syntax? Or, better still, an immigration hall. Papers arrive at a table, migrate to other tables or chairs, and, when they are rubber-stamped, get stuffed into drawers. By the way, outgoing mail on the floor. Observe the corner bookcase, the final catacomb – my file boxes. I like to forget.

Mrs Zut dropped to her knees near a window and was opening the bags.

Now (Pearson was offering his body to Zut), what would you like me to be or do? Stand here? Or there? Sit? Left leg crossed over right leg, right over left? Put on a look? Get a book at random? Open a drawer? Light a pipe? Talk? Think? Put hand on chin? Great Zut, make your wish known.

Talk, Zut. All photographers talk, put client at ease. Ask me questions. Dozens of pictures of me have been

taken. I could show you my early slim-subaltern-on-
the-Somme-waiting-to-go-over-the-top period. There
was my Popular Front look in the Thirties and Forties,
the jersey-wearing, all-the-world's-a-coal-mine period,
with close-ups of the pores and scars of the skin and the
gleam of sweat. There was the editorial look, when the
tailor had to let out the waist of my trousers, followed
by the successful smirk. In the Sixties the plunging
neckline, no tie. Then back to collar and tie in my
failed-bronze-Olympic period. Today I fascinate ar-
chaeologists – you know, the broken pillar of a lost
civilisation. Come on, Zut. What do you want?

Zut looked at the largest table. It had a clear space
among pots of pencils, ashtrays, paper clips, two piles
of folders for the execution block – a large blotter
embroidered by pen wipings, and on it was a board with
beautiful clean white paper clipped to it.

'There,' said Zut, pointing to the chair in front of it.
Zut had swollen veins on his long hands. 'Sit,' he said.

Pearson sat. There was a hiss from Mrs Zut's place
on the floor, close to Zut. She had pulled out the steel
rods of a whistling tripod. Zut gave a push to her
shoulder. Up came a camera. She screwed it on and
Zut fiddled with it, calling for more and more little
things. What fun you have in your branch of the trade,
said Pearson. You have little things to twizzle. Well, I
have paper clips, pipe cleaners, scissors, paste. I try out
pens, that's all – to save me from entering the wilderness, the wilderness of vocabulary.

But now Zut was pulling his creased jacket over his
head and squinting through the camera at Pearson, who

felt a small flake of his face fall off. And at that moment
Zut gave Mrs Zut a knock on her arm. 'Meter,' he said.
Then he let his coat slip back to his shoulders and stepped
from the end of the table to where Pearson was sitting
and held the meter, with shocking intimacy, close to
Pearson's head. He looked back at the window, muttering a word. Was the word 'unclean'? And he turned to
squint through the camera and looked up to say, 'Take
your glasses off.'

My glasses. My only defence. Can't see a thing. He
took them off.

Ah, Zut, I see you don't talk, because you are after
the naked truth, you are a dabbler in the puddles of the
mind. As you like, but I warn you I'm wise to that.

'Don't smile.'

I see, you're not a smile-please man, muttered Pearson. Oh, Zut, you've such a shriven look. If you take
me naked, you will miss all the *et cetera* of my life. I am
all *et cetera*. But Zut was back under his jacket, spying
again, and then he did something presumptuous. He
came out of his jacket, reached across the table, and
moved a pot of pencils out of the way. The blue pot,
that rather pretty *et cetera* that Pearson's wife had found
in a junk shop next to the butcher's – now a pizza café
– twenty-four years ago on a street not in this district.
Zut, you have moved a part of my life to another table,
it will hate being there, screamed Pearson's soul. How
dare you move my wife?

Anything else?

'Not necessary,' said Zut and, reaching out, gave Mrs

Zut a knock on the arm. 'Lamp,' he said between his teeth.

Mrs Zut scrabbled in the bag and pulled out a rubbery cord; at the end was a clouded yellow lamp, a small sickly moon. She stood up and held it high.

Zut gave another knock on her arm as he spied into the camera.

'Higher,' he said.

Up went the lamp. Another knock.

'Keep still. You're letting it droop,' said Zut. Oh, Florence Nightingale, can't you, after all these years, hold it steady?

'Look straight into the camera,' called Zut from under his jacket.

'Now write,' said Zut.

'Write? Where?'

'On that paper.'

'Pen or pencil?' said Pearson. 'Write what?'

'Anything.'

'Like at school.'

Pearson tipped the board on the edge of the table.

'Don't tip the board. Keep it flat.'

'I can't write flat. I never write flat,' Pearson said. And I never write in public, if anyone is in the room. I grunt. I make a noise.

I bet you can't photograph a noise.

Pearson glanced at Zut. Then, sulking, he slid the board back flat on the table and felt the room tip up.

Zut, Pearson murmured. I shall write: Zut keeps on hitting his wife. Zut keeps on hitting his wife. Can't write that. He might see. Zut, I am going to diddle you.

I shall write my address, 56 Hill Road Terrace, with the wrong post code – N6 4DN. Here goes: 56 Hill Road Terrace, 56 Hill Road Terrace . . .

'Keep on writing,' said Zut.

Pearson continued 56 Hill Road Terrace and then misspelled 'terrace'. Out of the corner of his eye he saw the little yellow lamp.

'Now look up at me,' said Zut.

The room tipped higher.

'Like that. Like that. Like that,' hissed Zut. 'Go on. Now go on writing.'

Click, click, click, went the shutter of the camera. A little toad in the lens has shot out a long tongue and caught a fly.

'You're dropping it again,' said Zut, giving Mrs Zut a punch.

'Good,' the passionate Zut called to Pearson, then came out of his jacket.

'My face has gone,' Pearson said.

But how do you know you've got *me?* My soul spreads all over my body, even in my feet. My face is nothing. At my age I don't need it. It is no more than a servant I push around before me. Or a football I kick ahead of me, taking all the blows, in shops, in the streets. It knows nothing. It just collects. I send it to smirk at parties, to give lectures. It has a mouth. I've no idea what it says. It calls people by the wrong names. It is an indiscriminate little grinner. It kisses people I've never met. The only time my face and I exchange a word is when I shave. Then it sulks.

Click, went the camera.

Pearson sat back and put down his pen and dropped his arm to his side.

'Will you do that again,' said Zut. 'The way you just dropped your arm,' Zut said.

Pearson did it.

'No,' said Zut. 'We've missed it.'

Pearson was hurt, and apologised to Mrs Zut, the dumb goddess. Not for worlds would he upset her husband. She simply gazed at Zut.

Zut himself straightened up. The room tipped back to its normal state. Pearson noticed the long lines down the sides of Zut's mouth, wondered why the jacket did not rumple his grey hair. Cropped, of course. How old was he? Where had he flown from? Hovering vulture. Unfortunate Satan walking up and down the world looking for souls. Satan on his treadmill. I bet your father was in, say, the clock trade, was it? – and when you were a boy you took his watch to pieces looking for Time. Why don't you *talk?* You're not like that man who came here last year and told me that he waited until he felt there was a magnetic flow uniting himself and me. A technological flirt. Nor are you like that other happy fellow with the waving fair hair who said he unselfed himself, forgot money, wife, children, all, for a few seconds to become me!

Zut slid a new plate into the camera and glanced up at the ceiling. It was smudged by the faint shadows of the beams behind it. A prison or cage effect. Why was he looking at the ceiling? Did he want it to be removed?

Pearson said, 'Painted only five years ago. And look at it! More expense.'

Zut dismissed this.

'Look towards the window,' said Zut.

'Which one?' said Pearson.

'On the right,' said Zut. 'Yes. Yes.' Another blow on that poor woman's arm.

'Lamp – higher. Still higher.'

Click, click from the toad in the lens.

'Again,' said Zut.

Click. Click. Another click.

'Ah!' said Zut, as if about to faint.

He's found something at last, Pearson thought. But, Zut, I bet you don't know where my mind was. No, I was not looking at the tree-tops. I was looking at a particular branch. On a still day like this, there is always one leaf skipping about at the end of a branch on its own while the rest of the tree is still. It has been doing that for years. Why? An *et cetera*, a distinguished leaf. Could be me. What am I but a leaf?

One more half-hearted click from the camera, and then Zut stood tall. He had achieved boredom.

'I've got all I want,' he muttered sharply to his wife.

All? said Pearson, appealing. There are tons of me left. I know I have a face like a cup of soup with handles sticking out – you know? – after it has been given a couple of stirs with a wooden spoon. A speciality in a way. What wouldn't I give for bone structure, a nose with bone in it!

Zut gave a last dismissive look around the room.

'That's it,' he said to his wife.

She started to dismantle the tripod. Zut walked to the photograph of the Albert Memorial on the chest near the door, done by another photographer, and studied it. There was an enormous elephant's head in the foreground. Zut pointed. 'Only one eye,' he said censoriously.

'The other's in shadow,' said Pearson.

'Elephants have two eyes,' said Zut. And then, 'Is there a . . .'

'Of course, of course, the door on the left.'

Pearson was putting the muscles of his face back in place. He was alone with Mrs Zut, who was packing up the debris of the hour.

'I have always admired your husband's work,' he said politely.

'Thank you,' she said from the floor, buckling the bags.

'Remarkable pictures of men – and, of course, women. I think I saw one of you, didn't I, in his last collection?'

'No,' she said from the floor, looking proud. 'I don't allow him to take my picture.'

'Oh surely –'

'No,' she said, the whole of herself standing up, full-faced, solid and human.

'His first wife, yes. Not me,' she said resolutely, killing the other in the ordinary course of life.

Then Zut came back, and in procession they all began thanking their way downstairs to the door.

At the exhibition Pearson sneaked in to see himself, stayed ten minutes to look at his portrait, and came out screaming, thinking of Mrs Zut.

An artist, he said. Herod! he was shouting. When the head of John the Baptist was handed to you on that platter, the eyes of that beautiful severed head were peacefully closed. But what do I see at the bottom of your picture. A high haunted room whose books topple. Not a room indeed, but a dank cistern or aquarium of stale water. No sparkling anemone there but the bald head of a melancholy frog, its feet clinging to a log, floating in literature. O Fame, cried Pearson, O Maupassant, O *Tales of Hoffmann*, O Edgar Allan Poe, O Grub Street.

Pearson rushed out and rejoined the human race on that bus going north and sat silently addressing the passengers, the women particularly, who all looked like Mrs Zut. The sight of them changed his mind. He was used, he said, to his face gallivanting with other ladies and gentlemen, in newspapers, books, and occasionally on the walls of galleries like that one down the street. Back down the street, he said, a man called Zut, a photographer, an artist, not one of your click-click men, had exhibited his picture, but by a mysterious accident of art had portrayed his soul instead of mine. What faces, Pearson said, that poor fellow must see just before he drops off to sleep at night beside the wise woman who won't let him take a picture of her, fearing perhaps the Evil Eye. A man in the image trade, like myself. Pearson called back as he got off the bus. Not a Zurbarán, more a Hieronymus Bosch perhaps. No one noticed Pearson getting off.

ABOUT THE AUTHOR

V. S. PRITCHETT was born in England in 1900. One of the great men of twentieth-century literature, Sir Victor is recognized as a formidable critic, novelist, writer of short stories, travel writer, autobiographer, and biographer. He was knighted in 1975 and is a foreign honorary member of the American Academy of Arts and Letters and of the Academy of Arts and Sciences. He lives in London with his wife, Dorothy.